What was Alex doing in Washington?

It was almost as if she'd known he couldn't stop thinking about their night together.

He stood as the door opened and Alex spilled into the room. Her face glowed and something seized his lungs as he stared at her. She'd stolen his ability to think simply by walking into the room. That was not supposed to happen.

Her eyes shone with unexpected moisture and he lost his place again. This wasn't a social visit, obviously. "Is something wrong?"

"Maybe." She hesitated, biting her lip in that way that said she didn't know what to say next.

If only he could take her in his arms and kiss her hello, like he wanted to. He sighed. "I like you a lot, Alex, but I'm not sure we're meant to continue our affair. It's complicated. And not your fault. I wish things could be different. And not so complicated."

She choked out a laugh that sounded a bit like a sob. "Yeah, I wish that, too. Unfortunately, things are far more complicated than you could ever dream."

"What—"

"I'm pregnant."

* * *

A Pregnancy Scandal is part of the Love and Lipstick series: For four female executives, mixing business with pleasure leads to love!

Dear Reader,

If you've read the first book in the Love and Lipstick quartet, *The CEO's Little Surprise*, you've met Alex. Awkward, shy, a bit straitlaced...and she doesn't wear makeup, despite being a quarter owner in a cosmetic company. I've loved her since the moment she first appeared in my head. What a study in contrasts she is. And what a heroine she turned out to be!

The makeover she gets in the epilogue of Cass's book lands Alex in the arms of the man she's been drooling over—Senator Phillip Edgewood. Gorgeous, charismatic, scandal-averse...and a widower to boot. What could Alex and Phillip possibly have in common other than explosive chemistry? They're about to find out when one night leads to a lifetime commitment in the form of an unexpected pregnancy. Alex shuns the spotlight. Phillip commands it. How will they work *this* out, especially when neither of them wants a marriage based on love?

I had the best time throwing these two together! Especially because pregnancy isn't the only surprise in store for either of them.

Don't miss the other three books in this series about Alex's friends and business partners. Love and Lipstick: four friends fall in love against the backdrop of the cosmetic company they created. Of course, it's never as simple as that! These friends deal with secrets, lies, corporate espionage and sabotage, none of which they'd dreamed would mix with makeup.

I love to hear from readers. Find out where to connect with me online at katcantrell.com.

Kat Cantrell

KAT CANTRELL

———

A PREGNANCY SCANDAL

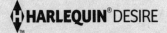

Recycling programs
for this product may
not exist in your area

ISBN-13: 978-0-373-73464-1

A Pregnancy Scandal

Copyright © 2016 by Kat Cantrell

Printed in U.S.A.

Kat Cantrell read her first Harlequin novel in third grade and has been scribbling in notebooks since then. She writes smart, sexy books with a side of sass. She's a former Harlequin So You Think You Can Write winner and an RWA Golden Heart® Award finalist. Kat, her husband and their two boys live in north Texas.

Books by Kat Cantrell

Harlequin Desire

Marriage with Benefits
The Things She Says
The Baby Deal
Pregnant by Morning
The Princess and the Player
Triplets Under the Tree
The SEAL's Secret Heirs

Happily Ever After, Inc.

Matched to a Billionaire
Matched to a Prince
Matched to Her Rival

Newlywed Games

From Ex to Eternity
From Fake to Forever

Love and Lipstick

The CEO's Little Surprise
A Pregnancy Scandal

Visit her Author Profile page at Harlequin.com, or katcantrell.com, for more titles.

To Anne Marsh for about a million reasons but mostly because you're always there on the other side of my chat window.

One

The third time Alex ducked behind the Greek statue, Senator Phillip Edgewood's curiosity got the best of him. Yeah, he'd been watching her from across the crowded room as she chatted with her friends and coworkers. How could he not?

Alexandra Meer was the most beautiful woman in the room.

Surprisingly so. Phillip had half expected her to show up to his fundraiser-slash-party in jeans, which he would not have minded in the slightest because he liked her no matter what she wore. But this dressed-up, made-up, trans-formed version of the woman he'd first met a couple of weeks ago at the Fyra Cosmetics corporate office—*wow.*

Senator Galindo cleared her throat, drawing Phillip's attention back to their conversation. Ramona Galindo, the other United States senator from Texas, and Phillip had a lot in common and they often socialized when they were both home in Dallas. But it was hard to focus on the senator with Alex's secretive actions going on. He pretended to listen, because the whole point of this evening was to network with his colleagues outside of Washington, while he also strained to catch a glimpse of Alex.

Was she covertly dumping canapés before anyone figured out she wasn't eating them? Or was she hoping to meet someone interesting in the shadowy recesses?

If it was the former, Phillip felt it was his civic duty to inform her that, while this was his party, he hated the canapés, too. If it was the latter, well, it might also be his civic duty to grant her wish.

Honestly, Phillip needed the distraction. Today was Gina's birthday. Or rather, it would have been. If his wife had lived, she would have been thirty-two. You'd think nearly two years of practice being a widower would afford a guy a better handle on the designation. But here he was, still stumbling through it.

And that decided it. He could spend the rest of the evening morose and moody. Or he could fan the sparks that always kicked up whenever he was around Alex. When Phillip had agreed to help Fyra Cosmetics navigate the FDA approval process for a new product, he'd never expected to meet someone so intriguing, especially not when that someone was the company's chief financial officer.

He and Alex had been developing a "thing" over late lunches and one-on-one meetings. She laughed at his jokes and made him feel like a man instead of a politician. And she'd come to this party stag when he'd been almost positive she'd decline. How much more of a hint did he need that their relationship might become more than two people working together?

"Excuse me," he murmured to Senator Galindo as he skirted her expertly, tugging on the white shirtsleeves under his tuxedo as he beelined across his cavernous living room to catch the most interesting woman at his party in the act of…whatever she was doing.

He crossed his arms and stepped behind the statue, boxing her in. The scent of Alex overwhelmed him first… light, fruity…and then the woman did. He let both wake up his blood. Which didn't take long.

"Fancy meeting you here," he said blithely. "I hope I'm not the bore at this party that you're avoiding."

Alex's eyes widened and then warmed dangerously fast. Her eyes were the most fascinating shade of green with a little brown dot in the left iris that he couldn't help but notice. She was easily the most distinctive woman he'd ever met, and that was saying something when he regularly mixed with the elite of both Dallas and Washington.

"No, of course not. You couldn't pry that title away from the mayor with a crowbar." And then she groaned, which made him grin. "I mean, I'm not avoiding the mayor. And he's not a bore. Neither are you! I'm not avoiding anyone."

Was it wrong that he enjoyed flustering her so much? It was so easy to do and she always said something outrageous that never failed to make him smile. He needed to smile, especially tonight. And she was the only person in attendance who had managed that feat. The only person he'd met in a long time who seemed unimpressed by his position or wealth. He liked that.

"But if you *were* hoping to avoid someone, this would be the opportune spot." He leaned against the wall and crossed one ankle over the other. "No one would know you were back here unless they were already watching you."

The shadows weren't deep enough to cover her blush. "You were watching me?"

"Oh, come now." He tsked. "When a woman wears a dress like that, surely it's not a shock that a man would spend a great deal of time looking at her."

She glanced down and scowled.

"It's just a dress," she mumbled.

No, it was anything but. The off-white dress had a hint of gold sparkle that caught the light when she moved, and the fabric draped over her curves in a way that announced she had some. That was news to Phillip and he'd call that a front-page story, because she was an amazingly beautiful woman already, even before this evening's transformation.

But *with* the transformation...well, she'd captured his interest thoroughly, because he hoped it meant she wasn't averse to the occasional dress-up event. Politicians attended a lot of those and Phillip had a huge void in the plus-one category.

Maybe he'd found a potential candidate.

"Yet I've never seen you in a dress." He raised one eyebrow in emphasis, which she did not miss. "I've come by Fyra for FDA meetings, what, like three or four times? And you, my dear, have reinvented the concept of casual wear. Cass, Trinity and Harper always wear suits, but you're most often in jeans."

The other three cofounders of Fyra dressed well and without regard to price tags. Phillip appreciated a woman who knew her way around a stylist, and normally he would have said he preferred a sophisticated woman. Gina had never met a rack at Nordstrom she could leave untouched, and the small handful of women he'd preoccupied himself with after Gina died could only be described as high maintenance. He'd lost interest in them pretty quickly.

But Alex...well, Alex intrigued him. She'd instantly stood out from her three counterparts when his cousin Gage had introduced Phillip to the founders of Fyra Cosmetics.

He couldn't ignore the demure, brown-haired woman clad in a T-shirt, hair scraped back into a ponytail. It was baffling to walk into a meeting with Fyra's executives and see the chief financial officer's face bereft of makeup. It would be like introducing himself to someone as Senator Phillip Edgewood and then claiming he had no interest in the laws of the United States.

He was intrigued. He wanted to know her better. Understand why he couldn't stop thinking about her. Why she was so different from any woman of his acquaintance. But he had to tread carefully with the opposite sex for so many reasons, not the least of which was his aversion to scandal. And then there was the other thing: he was on the lookout for a permanent plus one. Only the right woman would do for that role and his criteria were stringent.

No point in getting a woman's hopes up unless he filled them. He didn't know if Alex fell in that category or not, but he planned to find out.

"Don't you have guests?" she asked and glanced over his shoulder. "I'm keeping you from them."

"Seventy-eight, if I recall." Yes, he should be doing host-type things, definitely. He didn't move. "And you're one of my guests, as well. I'd be remiss if I didn't see to your welfare as you skulk about behind this very large statue."

"My dress is…uncomfortable." She waved at her torso. "None of this stays in place like it's supposed to."

Naturally, his eye was drawn to the area in question. "Looks like everything is in order to me."

"Because I just adjusted it all," she hissed fiercely.

The image of Alex ducking behind his statue to dip her hands under her dress to *adjust things* flooded through his senses, unchecked. He couldn't unsee it. Couldn't unexperience it. And now this small space in the corner wasn't nearly big enough to hold a senator, a CFO and the enormous attraction sizzling between them.

He stopped himself from asking if she needed help adjusting anything else. It was right there on the tip of his tongue. But United States senators didn't run around saying whatever they felt like, no matter how badly he wanted to flirt with her. Among other things.

Phillip's life was not his own, never had been, nor would he have it any other way. He was an Edgewood, born into a long line of statesmen, and an even longer line of Texas oilmen, and his family was counting on him to be the first one to make it to the White House.

To accomplish that, he needed a wife, plain and simple. A single president hadn't been elected in the United States since the eighteen hundreds. The problem was that his heart still belonged to Gina, and he'd met few women willing to play second fiddle to another woman, even one who'd passed away.

The catch-22 was brutal. Either he'd marry someone in name only and make his peace with loneliness for the next fifty years or hope that he magically stumbled over a woman who was okay with his ground rules for marriage— friends and lovers, sure. But love wasn't on offer. It would feel like a betrayal of the highest order.

It wasn't fair; he knew that. But Phillip didn't believe in second chances. No one got lucky enough to find their soul mate twice. But if Alex was the right woman for him, she'd understand.

Instead of the dozens of other offers he'd have rather issued, he asked, "Would you like a glass of champagne?"

"Do I look that much like I need a drink?" she asked wryly. "Or are you a mind reader?"

He grinned. "Neither. I thought it was a shame you were stuck back here in the corner with your dress problems and couldn't enjoy the party."

Tucking an errant lock of hair behind her ear, an escapee from her upswept hairdo, she rolled her eyes. "It'll take a lot more than champagne to get me to enjoy a black-tie party."

There she went again with her outrageous statements. He smiled. "Should I be insulted that my party isn't up to par?"

A horrified light dawned in her expression. "No! Your party is perfect because, well…you're *you* and your house is amazing and the guests are great. I'm just clumsy with small talk. Obviously."

She blinked up at him from under her lashes. On any other woman, that look would have been coquettish, designed to convey blatant invitation, and he would have walked away without regret. On her, it was a hint of vulnerability, of uncertainty. And together, they unexpectedly whacked him in the heart.

Hadn't seen that coming. His attraction had deepened over a simple look.

"Not clumsy," he corrected smoothly. "Honest. That's refreshing."

"I'm glad someone thinks so." She scowled, but it was cute on her. "Numbers people like me are not usually sought out by party hosts. We tend to skulk about behind statues and embarrass ourselves with wardrobe problems."

"Why did you come to the party if you don't like dressing up?"

Obviously she hadn't morphed into someone who liked black-tie affairs, which was a shame. She was looking less and less like a candidate for his permanent plus one. The problem was, the more he stood here with her, the more he wanted to chuck all his marriage rules.

"You know why."

The undercurrents between them heated as their gazes locked. He couldn't have walked away from Alex if his ancestral home caught fire. He was close enough to see the brown fleck in her eye and it was oddly intimate. His attraction to her was ungodly strong and a colossal problem.

"You came for me?" he asked, but it wasn't really a question. Her smile answered affirmatively anyway. "I'm flattered you'd put on an uncomfortable dress and wear makeup just for me."

"Call it a rare burst of spontaneity. Totally unlike me. But hopefully worth it in the end."

He almost groaned. She was killing him. Why couldn't they be two normal people meeting at a party, with no agenda other than to spend time together? "I'm a fan of spontaneous women."

Especially since he didn't have nearly enough opportunity to indulge in spontaneity. It was the enemy of someone eyeing the presidency. His life consisted of carefully worded statements and planned appearances, strenuously vetted acquaintances and photo ops. The chances of, say, happening across an intriguing woman in a shadowy corner were nearly nil.

Yet here he was. They shared an inability to be spontaneous. Just this once, he wanted to indulge in spontaneity alongside her. Maybe they *could* be two people who met at a party and had fun with no expectations.

His grin widened. This was probably the most he'd smiled without being ordered to in…a long time. "Let's do something totally impulsive, then. Dance with me."

As vigorously as she shook her head, it was a wonder it didn't roll off her neck. Brown, glossy strands floated from her hairdo, drifting down around her face. "I can't dance with you in front of all these people."

"You can so. Your dress is appropriately adjusted. You're over the age of eighteen and not married."

That was the trifecta of scandal potentials and the three he always checked off the list automatically within the first half a second in a woman's company. After his uncle had lost his Senate nomination over some risqué pictures starring a woman who was not his wife, Phillip had vowed to stay on the straight and narrow.

His career wasn't just about the election but about making a difference. Changing the world. He refused to allow his star to be snuffed out early for any reason, least of all a woman. His life was privileged, no doubt, but with that privilege came great responsibility.

"This dress doesn't have magical powers, Phillip. I'm clumsy with words *and* feet."

"You don't seem to realize that you're a successful executive who cofounded a million-dollar company. You should be out on the dance floor, intimidating the hell out of all the people here because you are Alexandra Meer and you don't care what they think."

He held out his hand. There was no way he would let her spend the night in the corner. They were going to honor her spontaneous impulse to attend this party. Of course, that was just an excuse. He couldn't help but steal a few more minutes of her company.

Alex hesitated, staring at Phillip's outstretched hand.

She'd been hiding behind the statue for a reason. Other women must have some kind of special sticky skin that allowed them to wear strapless dresses without falling out of them. Alex didn't. Dancing would make everyone else aware of it, too.

"Come on," he pleaded in his deep voice that made her shiver tonight as much as it had the first time she'd heard it. "I can't leave you back here, and if you don't dance with me, I'll be an absentee host at my own party. This is my house. It would seem weird."

Alex glanced at the very large, very ugly statue she'd taken refuge behind. "You weren't supposed to see me."

No one was; that was the point. The statue was a great place to hide but still allowed her to sort of be in the midst of things. Parties always reminded her of why she didn't attend them. Social niceties were a confusing, complex set of rules that she could never seem to follow. Alex liked rules. But only when they made sense, like in finance. Numbers were the same yesterday and today as they would be tomorrow.

Normally, she followed her own number one rule to the letter—stay out of the spotlight. But she'd developed a fierce attraction to Phillip and, well…parties seemed to be his natural habitat. Thus she had to attend one to see if things might heat up between them outside of Fyra. Because there were sparks between them, but he'd yet to make a move. She wanted to find out if his glacial pace had to do with lack of interest or something else.

Cass had bullied her into a makeover and pried Alex's credit card out of her fingers to purchase this dress. It all felt very surreal and a little like trying too hard. Alex didn't have a glamorous bone in her body, but the resulting image in her mirror had turned out pretty good, if she did say so herself.

And here she and Phillip were, flirting and having fun, and he'd just asked her to dance. This dress *did* have magical powers.

Maybe she *could* dance with him. Just once. Then she'd slink back to her hiding spot before someone else tried to talk to her. Someone who wasn't as understanding as Phillip about her permanent foot-in-mouth syndrome.

Slowly, she reached out. It was almost harder to do that than it had been to walk through Phillip's palatial double front doors, knowing he was on the other side, divinely, devastatingly handsome. Actually, just about everything she'd done in the name of advancing her relationship with Phillip had taken a huge amount of bravery.

Maybe the stars had finally aligned to alleviate the loneliness Alex had been feeling lately—a by-product of both social awkwardness and a firm belief that romance was a myth perpetuated by the retail market. She dated here and there. Not often, for obvious reasons. But she liked companionship as much as the next girl, and Phillip was the first man in a long time that she couldn't stop thinking about.

Tonight was about seeing where things might go between them.

Except, this hundred-year-old house was overwhelming—with a grand foyer the size of a public library, flanked by two curved staircases reaching toward the second floor. It was a visual reminder of his elite status and that men like him lived a whole different kind of existence, one that was ill-suited for a quiet wallflower like Alex.

But when her flesh connected with Phillip's, it was a shock to her system. Need lanced through her. *Hello. Been a long time since those muscles had a workout, yes sirree.*

Their gazes collided and his hot blue eyes spoke to her, saying without words that he wanted her, too. Well, how about that?

She let it sing through her because men never noticed her. Alex had perfected the art of fading into the background, but Phillip had never overlooked her. Her reaction was powerful and visceral.

"Alex," he murmured and tightened his grip on her hand. "We have to dance now. Otherwise, something very bad might happen."

"Like what?" she asked curiously. His gaze was on her lips as if he might lean forward at any moment and take her mouth with his.

That sounded very *good* to her.

Maybe he'd even back her up farther into the corner and do it properly. His hands were smooth and strong, and she'd fantasized about them as they'd sat through long meetings together.

It wasn't a crime. Just because she didn't buy into the fantasy about love and romance didn't mean she had an aversion to sex.

She'd been dreaming of kissing him for weeks, ever since the first time he'd walked into Fyra. The sparks between them had been instant and deliciously hot. And their connection was more than just physical. He was thoughtful, well-spoken, listened to her ideas and had a wicked sense of humor. She genuinely liked him. The insane gorgeousness attached to his personality was just a big, fat bonus.

"Bad, like I might show every last person at this party to the door," he said. "And focus on no one but you."

Heat kicked up in her midsection. Oh, yes, to have all that delicious focus on her. He had this way of making her feel like the only person in the room, even when there were a hundred present.

It was an invitation. And a question. Where did she want this evening to lead?

Where did *he* want this evening to lead?

Were they on the same page about what their association might look like afterward? They were working together, after all. Not everyone could do that and become personally involved. That was where the romantics messed it all up. Relationships were black-and-white and easy to navigate as long as you didn't let yourself get bogged down in unquantifiable emotions. Her parents' divorce had been nasty enough to prove that love was one of the worst illusions ever invented.

She should probably feel him out about their future interaction before letting him do bad things to her. Also, he'd thrown this party for a reason, which would not be accomplished by allowing him to throw everyone out. It would be terrible of her to force him to end it early because she was a giant chicken about dancing in public.

More bravery needed, stat. "Let's dance."

"This way, Ms. Meer."

He led her to the dance floor and pulled her into his arms.

The crowd dynamic shifted instantly as people checked out the woman dancing with the senator. Alex's back heated with the scrutiny. The only friendly faces in the crowd were her boss, Cassandra, and Cass's fiancé, Gage, who was Phillip's cousin.

Self-consciousness turned Alex's feet into lead.

"Right here, Alex." Phillip tapped his temple and let his hand drift back to her waist. "Keep your eyes on me. Don't worry about them. They don't exist."

Ha. If only that were true. Of course, she'd had her chance to make that a reality when he'd offered to kick everyone out. She had no doubt that if she'd taken him up on his invitation, the crowd would already be in their chauffeured limousines heading for home.

Why hadn't she taken him up on it, again?

She did as instructed, locking her gaze to his molten-blue eyes. He swirled her around the hardwood floor to the tempo of the classical music piping through his expensive, invisible sound system. The crowd faded away and she became so very aware of his hands on her body, exactly as she'd envisioned them. Well, not exactly. In the majority of her fantasies, they were both naked.

Heat flushed her skin, arrowing straight to her core as he watched her closely.

"See?" he murmured. "Better."

Yes. This night, this man holding her in his arms. All better. It wasn't the dress, but *Phillip* who held the magical powers. She was someone else when she was with him, someone who didn't have to fade into the woodwork to avoid making a fool of herself. Someone who could be with a man like Phillip and it made sense, even though they were social opposites.

And she very much wanted to take advantage of the magic while it lasted. Maybe she could, just for tonight.

Two

Phillip didn't leave Alex's side all night.

It was both sweet and intoxicating. She lost all track of time and place, forgetting about the judgmental audience as Phillip had entreated her to do. He was an amazing man who made her feel special. Her starving soul ate up the attention and begged for more.

She could get used to being the center of Phillip's world. Used to how the focused glint in his blue eyes pulled on strings deep inside. Used to how her heart seemed lighter when he—

A tap on her shoulder startled her. She glanced backward. *Cass.* Alex had nearly forgotten her friend was at the party.

"Ms. Claremont." Phillip nodded to Cass without missing a beat. "My apologies for failing to tell you how stunning you look this evening. Gage is a lucky man."

"Yeah, you've been way too busy to notice me," Cass

said, tongue in cheek. "I'll be sure to let Gage make it up to me later."

Alex thought about smacking her but that would mean removing her hands from Phillip's shoulders.

"I need to borrow Alex for a minute," Cass explained, and Alex nearly sobbed as Phillip's arms dropped from around her.

Cass dragged Alex to the powder room, nodding and making nice to a couple of Hollywood types who were leaving as they walked up. The glitterati lived in a world she wasn't a part of and Alex had no idea who the glamorous women were. Cass not only knew them by name, she belonged in a roomful of beautiful people who never said the wrong thing.

Not that Alex was jealous. It was just fact. She loved the CEO of Fyra like a sister. After all, Cass had insisted on Alex taking over the financial joystick of Fyra despite full knowledge of the teenage rebellion that had landed Alex in a courtroom, staring down the barrel of jail time.

That ledger in her head would never balance. She owed Cass for taking a chance on her and she'd gladly bury herself in Fyra's numbers until the day she died, if necessary.

But that didn't mean Alex forgave the interruption.

"What was so important?" she muttered as soon as the door to the powder room closed, affording them a measure of privacy. "I was dancing."

Cass raised her perfectly penciled eyebrows. "Yes, you were. But Gage and I are ready to go."

"Already?" Alex had caught a ride with them since Gage had insisted there was plenty of room in his chauffeured town car. On the drive over, she'd been contemplating how she would get home when she sneaked out early from the party. She'd been sure attending Phillip's shindig would go down as the worst idea she'd ever had. Funny how that had turned out.

"It's midnight." Cassandra pointed at the ornate wall clock for emphasis. "We have a son who can't tell time and will be up at 6:00 a.m."

Dismayed, Alex stared at the clock, willing it to be a few hours earlier. The hands didn't change position. Why did it have to be midnight? This night should never end because in the morning, she'd go back to being invisible.

"You just hired a nanny," Alex reminded Cass with a touch of desperate logic. "Can't she get up with Robbie?"

This was a bizarre conversation. Robbie was Gage Branson's son from a previous relationship and never would Alex have taken Cass for the type to willingly enter a relationship with a single father. But she and Gage were deliriously happy. It was so optimistic of them to fall in love despite all the complications. Alex hoped they'd defy the odds and have a long, happy life together.

Cass shook her head with a laugh. "I like to get up with him when I can, since Gage and I still live in different cities for the time being. If you want to stay, just say so and catch a cab later."

That was Cassandra. A problem solver. "I can't stay."

Fyra's newest shade of lipstick appeared from the depths of Cass's sparkly bag. She slicked it over her lips and puckered before asking, "Why not?"

Because the thought of staying without the safety net of her friend induced a swirly feeling in Alex's stomach that could easily turn into full-blown panic. This was a party. The place where Alex was the least comfortable.

And while she'd danced with Phillip, she still had no idea how he intended the evening to end. What if she'd misread his signals? It wasn't like she had a lot of practice.

Then there was the soft gush inside every time he laughed

at one of her jokes or did something gallant. Those were things she could never get enough of. The fact that she liked them so much was probably the best reason of all to disentangle herself before things progressed. When a man got that far under her skin so quickly, it could only lead to trouble.

"Phillip and I have no business getting involved," Alex explained lamely.

"Honey, you and Phillip are already *involved*." Cass accompanied the word with exaggerated air quotes, an impressive feat considering she still had the tube of lipstick in her hand. "Whether you like it or not. He is the whole reason you came. You like Phillip and want to see where it goes. Right? Otherwise, why did I spend all that time coaxing you into that dress?"

Alex could hear herself being ridiculous. "I do like Phillip, but—"

"Is this about your mom again? Because, honey, she's not you. Just because your dad was a weasel doesn't mean all men are."

Alex closed her mouth. Yeah, her parents' divorce had a lot to do with her caution, but Cass never seemed to understand how deeply it had hurt Alex. How it had driven so many of her decisions, then and now. After all, Alex had a juvenile arrest record thanks to a pathetic attempt to get back at her parents for splitting up. Later, after her mom had patiently straightened Alex out, she'd realized things weren't as black-and-white as she'd assumed. That was why it never paid to get emotional over a relationship. Love was too messy and complicated.

It was much better to fade into the woodwork and focus on the numbers parading across Fyra's balance sheet.

A wave of sensation sloshed through her stomach. Definitely panic.

"Do you want to stay?" Cass asked point-blank. There was no mistaking what she was really asking.

Staying meant she was giving Phillip the green light. He'd been eyeing her all night like a gentleman, never pushing her, but it didn't take a rocket scientist to figure out that the senator wanted more than a dance. Alex was being silly even questioning that.

If it had been anyone other than Cass, she'd lie. "I do. But I'm not—"

"Yes, you are." Firmly, Cass took Alex by the shoulders. In heels, she and Cass were almost the same height. "You're making this too hard. No one is asking you to marry him. This is about right now, that man and what you want. Go after him."

Alex's insides settled a bit.

It sounded so simple. Don't worry about things she couldn't control and just enjoy the attention of a man she'd been salivating over for weeks. Don't assume he cared about anything other than sex—better yet, make it hot enough that he lost all interest in anything other than how good they could make each other feel. What would be the harm in a brief fling with a man she had a not-so-secret crush on? The magic didn't have to end at midnight.

A shiver rocked her shoulders. It had been a long time since she'd had sex that didn't require batteries, and Phillip would do just fine as reintroduction to the pleasures of a flesh-and-blood man. After all, he was a prime member of the species.

"Tell Gage I said good-night," Alex said decisively. "I have a senator to seduce."

Alex had been gone for five minutes and already a line of people had formed with Important, Pressing Matters to discuss with Phillip. One of those people was his father, whom he hadn't seen outside of Washington in over a week. Rarely did their paths cross anyway since his dad was a member of the House. They'd been discussing a secret energy project, but frankly, he couldn't concentrate on anything Congressman Robert Edgewood was saying as Phillip strained for a glimpse of the woman whose company he wasn't nearly finished enjoying.

That shimmering dress appeared in his peripheral vision. About time. A humming sense of anticipation kicked up, the same sense he'd had all evening as he immersed himself in Alexandra Meer. What had started out as a way to get to know her better had grown into something more. Something with teeth, which had clamped onto him.

He extracted himself from his dad with a very polite "Excuse me."

He drew up beside Alex, far too close. All of the other guests vanished. He tilted his head toward her ear and the scent of sweet pears made him hungry. Would it be awful if he tasted her?

He resisted. Barely. This woman had been in his arms all night, exactly what he'd needed to quit dwelling on Gina, and now he wanted Alex back against him, even if all they did was more socially approved dancing. He liked being around her, liked the way she made him feel. Of course, he'd be okay with whatever she dictated for the night's conclusion, but the sharp ache in his midsection reminded him that this woman could ease it, quite well.

"You're right," he murmured and eyed a spot he'd like to nuzzle, right along her jaw. "The mayor is a bore."

"I tried to tell you." She laughed softly, leaning into his space.

"Come with me," he said. "I have something I want to show you."

Suddenly eager to have some privacy, he led her upstairs

to a balcony that overlooked the living room. His grandfather had given him the Edgewood ancestral home in Old Preston Hollow as an engagement present with many of the original furnishings intact. An antique love seat hugged the back wall, far enough away from the wrought iron banister to hide them from prying eyes below.

Phillip had never appreciated the decor as much as he did at that moment. Hand to her back, he settled in next to her on the cushion. "You can see the whole bottom floor from here. But they can't see us."

"Handy." Then she cleared her throat. "Gage and Cass are leaving. They're my ride."

Disappointment walloped him. That sounded decidedly final. Had he misinterpreted the long heated glances? He'd just got her where he wanted her. Well, closer to where he wanted her, anyway.

"You're ditching me already?" he asked and tried to keep his voice light.

Probably for the best. What could possibly happen between them? A brief but satisfying interlude where he'd eventually have to say goodbye? A woman like Alex deserved promises he could never make. He would treat her well, of course, but if a woman got intimate with a man, she eventually wanted to fall in love and get married and have the whole heart of her mate. Phillip couldn't do that, didn't want to do that.

Gina had been enough for him. Sometimes the sadness of losing her overwhelmed him. Like it had today. Alex had distracted him and he was grateful.

But once the party ended, the cavernous house would seem even emptier. He was not looking forward to it.

Alex glanced up at him through her lashes, and her lips parted slightly. "Actually, I was wondering if you'd mind giving me a ride home. Later."

Later was a word he liked a whole lot. It held all sorts of interesting possibilities. A smile tugged at his mouth. "My car is available to you at any hour."

"Looks like the party is breaking up," she commented, and it took him a second to tear his gaze from her beautiful face to register what she meant.

He glanced down through the spindles. His living room had grown surprisingly empty. What time was it? He'd lost track of everything—the hour, his guests, the people he should have been entertaining. And now he was going to kick out the stragglers in under a minute like a bad host. Even worse, he was going to have his butler do it.

Phillip signaled to George, who'd been ushering guests out the door and coordinating with the valet. His butler had worked for the Edgewoods for over forty years, largely owing to his singular talent of being able to read minds. George nodded and began moving to the remaining groups of people, herding them toward the double front doors.

Phillip should probably care about that more. "Perfect timing, I'd say."

"I agree. I was looking forward to having you all to myself."

A current of awareness passed between them, zigzagging through his groin, waking up his body.

"Unless," she continued, "you'd rather I go?"

"Why would you think that?" It might have come out a little too forcefully.

She bit her lip, drawing it between her teeth. A habit he'd noticed she fell into when she was trying to decide what to say, not that he spent an inordinate amount of time staring at her mouth. Okay, probably more time than he should spend on it, but the meetings they'd had about the FDA approval process had been interminable and she'd been right there across the table.

"Just checking. I'm not the best at reading people."

All at once, he realized what she was fishing for.

He cupped her face. Her green eyes blazed with something warm, hopeful and slightly hungry. Even the brown dot seemed extravibrant under his scrutiny. For some reason, that sent a shaft of unadulterated desire through his gut.

"Tonight is about being spontaneous," he told her. "Neither of us is good at that. That means no expectations. Make it about what *you* want."

And he meant that seriously. If she wanted to talk all night, that was okay. Of course, he wouldn't turn down a willing woman in his bed. But he just wanted to spend time with her, realizing it was selfish. Realizing he couldn't offer her much. Realizing he should definitely aim his search for a wife of convenience in another direction.

But no expectations meant he didn't have to think about any of that, either. Not tonight.

"No expectations," she repeated and her smile grew. "I like that. I like that you get I have a hard time with being spontaneous. But I want to make it about what we *both* want. You know, assuming we both want the same thing."

His own smile widened. "I hope so."

A great, no-strings evening together. In whatever form that took.

"It won't be weird? Tomorrow? We are still working together," she reminded him. "Some people find it difficult to face each other over a boardroom table after getting naked together."

Okay, then. Now there was no question about whether they were on the same page. The burn in his loins flared hotter as he slid his hand to the back of her neck, drawing her close so he could feel for the pins.

He extracted one and let it fall. He'd been thinking

about doing that since their first moment on the dance floor. Now he could.

"Not weird," he murmured. "What happens at Phillip's house stays at Phillip's house."

With a shiver, she shook her head, loosening the pins under his questing fingers. He found them one by one, flicking them free. She tipped up her chin to pierce him with her gaze, and he fell into it as her hair rained down around her shoulders.

"Can I tell you a secret?" Her voice had gone husky.

He loved that he could affect her. "Anything."

"I sometimes lose track of the discussion in those meetings because I'm thinking about kicking everyone out and letting you kiss me. Maybe up against the table."

He groaned as that image slammed into his mind unencumbered because there was no blood left in his head to stop it. He understood her problem perfectly. "I generally lose my place because I'm thinking about what you taste like. Here."

Tracing the line of her throat starting from her ear, he slid a finger to her collarbone and replaced his finger with his mouth. Her flavor filled his senses as he fulfilled the fantasy of savoring it. Straining closer, she moaned and it was better than music.

He needed more. More contact. More music. More Alex. He drew her closer, nearly into his lap, and her dress came up over her hip as his palm gathered it. She pressed into his touch, arching into him.

And then somehow, she rolled and landed *in* his lap, straddling him. Wordlessly—because he couldn't have spoken if his life had depended on it—he cupped her rear, nestling her so their bodies aligned, and then her mouth crashed into his. The kiss ignited inside him, pounding adrenaline through his body, pumping euphoria along all his nerve endings.

More. Somehow she heard him or he communicated it telepathically because her mouth opened over his as she rolled her hips in a sensuous rhythm against the fiercest erection he'd experienced in recent memory. Maybe ever.

Heat broke over him like a blast from a detonated bomb, coalescing at the point of contact between their bodies, nearly finishing him off before they'd scarcely started. He tore his mouth from hers, panting.

"Wait," he murmured and stood with her in his arms. She clamped her legs around his waist and he stumbled to his bedroom blindly as she fastened her lips on his throat, sucking with erotic pulls that drove him insane.

"That's not the definition of *waiting*," he told her hoarsely and let her slide to the ground as he slammed the door shut with one foot.

"I'm not very patient." To prove it, she half turned and presented the zipper to her dress.

He reached out and pulled it. That glittery fabric snaked from her body and landed in a heap around her ankles as she spun back to face him. She was naked, and her high, peaked breasts called to him.

A curse worked itself loose from his mouth. "Are you trying to kill me?"

"No, I'm trying to get you into bed. Apparently I'm doing it wrong since you're still dressed."

Laughing around the raging desire clogging his throat, he stripped and scooped her up, then complied with her directive, depositing her gently on the bed. He rolled into her, and that fragrant, fruity scent encompassed him just as completely as the woman did.

"I've been fantasizing about this moment for a long time," she confessed. Her honesty tripped something inside him.

Honeyed warmth spread through his chest as they stared

at each other. This wasn't supposed to be anything other than two people connecting with no expectations. Guess that wasn't even possible with someone as unique as Alexandra Meer. She pulled things from deep inside that he'd have sworn were frozen. Things he didn't want to feel for another woman. But it was hard to shut down.

He liked her. She was smart and successful with a touch of vulnerability that set her apart from other women in his path. That had been true from the first moment he'd met her.

He might as well admit the same. "Me too."

Phillip kissed her and she slid a long, smooth leg between his, teasing, tempting and torturing all at once, and that was it. This wasn't going to happen slowly. He wanted her as badly as she seemed to want him.

He fumbled in the nightstand for some condoms he was pretty sure were still in there from the last time he'd brought a woman home maybe eight months ago. A year? He had a bad moment when he couldn't find them and then his fingers closed around one.

He tore it open and somehow got it on in one shot and then she was back in place against him, her gorgeous, sweet body aligned with his. After an eternity, he pushed inside and they joined in a clash of bodies that felt so right, Phillip could hardly stand it. She was unbelievably lush and sensuous.

They moved in a timeless rhythm that somehow became new and electrifying. She gave as much as she took and his mind drained of everything except returning the pleasure. Higher and higher they spiraled as her moans spurred him on. Their simultaneous climax was like icing on an already lip-smacking cake.

He held her quaking body tight against his as the release blasted through him. And then he couldn't let go. She smelled like pears and well-loved woman, and he craved her heat, even in the aftermath. Usually he preferred to recover on his own, but he still couldn't get enough of this amazing woman.

Sure, he'd wanted her, but sex wasn't the be-all, end-all. He'd wanted to explore the connection they'd both felt from the very first. It had been just as amazing as he'd hoped. But he'd anticipated burning off that attraction and moving on. Epic fail in that regard. He wasn't close to done and that felt like a problem.

He had to get her out of his bed before he started rehearsing a pretty speech designed to convince her to spend the night. Which was enough of a warning to scramble from the sheets. He had never *slept* with a woman other than Gina. Tonight was not the night to start.

Later, he drove Alex home in his Tesla instead of sending her with his driver, Randy, like he'd planned. He couldn't seem to let her go. The night had ended far too soon.

And though he couldn't give her everything she deserved, he didn't want to let Alex walk out of his life.

Just because they'd said no expectations didn't mean he couldn't ask to see her again. After all, he didn't really *know* what she was looking for in a relationship. How could he say what he had to offer wasn't enough if they didn't talk about it?

At the door of Alex's house just north of Dallas in University Park, he kissed her good-night and then pulled back to gorge himself on the sight of her beautiful face. Tomorrow, she'd go back to T-shirt-and-jeans Alex.

He wanted to see her again, no matter what she was wearing.

"Can I call you?" he asked hoarsely and cleared his throat. "Let me take you to dinner."

She smiled. "I'd like that."

Phillip mentally flipped through his calendar and then cursed. He'd fly to Washington tomorrow and hadn't planned to be back in Dallas for the foreseeable future. "I can't set a firm date. But please know it's not because I don't want to. I have to be in Washington. Duty calls."

"Phillip, no expectations." She cupped his face with both palms and held it. "I like spending time with you. But I'm not going to wait by the phone for you to call. I have a company to run. I'm busy, too. Call me when you're free."

A bit blindsided, he stared at her. Most women—*all* women he'd ever met—wouldn't have considered giving him a pass like that. Alex was something else. "That's very gracious."

She shrugged. "You're worth waiting for."

Something turned over in his heart. This was crazy. Instead of exploring their attraction and getting it out of their systems, he was trying to figure out how to juggle his schedule so he could see her again. He should be running back to his car and driving away very fast in pursuit of someone who was much better suited to being the wife he needed.

The wife he needed would understand he couldn't be disloyal to Gina. The wife he needed would stand by his side as he navigated the Washington social scene, wearing couture and cosmetics with ease. The wife he needed would understand that his career might require sacrifices to her own career.

Above all, the wife he needed would not generate all of these unexpected, confusing emotions. Alex was not what he needed.

His career was everything to him. It had saved him from drowning in grief two years ago, and with his eye on the White House, Alex would only complicate his life. No, she wasn't what he needed—but she was everything he wanted. And that made her very dangerous indeed.

Three

Four weeks later...

The packaging on the pregnancy test was too slick for Alex's shaking fingers to grip. Gracelessly, she stuck the end in her mouth and tore it open. The slim stick fell out and tumbled end over end into the toilet bowl with a splash. Of course.

This was surreal. The walls of the company she'd co-founded surrounded her. Fyra was a multimillion-dollar cosmetics powerhouse that she'd worked tirelessly to manage alongside her friends and partners. Every single dollar of revenue and every dime of expense had passed through her fingers from day one. She was responsible for hundreds of employees' paychecks.

And she couldn't do a simple thing like open plastic packaging.

"What happened?" Cass's voice rang out from the other side of the bathroom stall.

"I'm nauseous and clumsy," Alex shot back. "The stupid test made a break for it and landed in the water."

This was not the way Alex wanted to spend her lunch break.

She was pretty sure the test would only confirm what she already knew in her heart to be the truth. The upset stomach she'd been battling for over a week had nothing to do with the seafood she'd eaten last Friday and everything to do with the night she'd spent with Phillip.

"Can you get it out?"

"I'm working on it."

Liar. Staring at the little white stick down in the water wasn't solving the problem. Alex thought about just flushing the thing and avoiding the whole question of why no amount of prayer had started her skipped period. She and Phillip had used protection. This wasn't supposed to be happening.

"Just pee in the toilet," Cass suggested. "You don't have to be holding the stick for it to work."

Alex sighed and gave in to the inevitable. "Fine. It's done. Now, how long do I have to wait?"

"I don't know." Cass rustled the paper instructions she'd been holding when Alex had locked herself in the bathroom stall. "Three minutes."

Might as well be three hours. Alex shredded her nails in under a minute and a half, not that it mattered. No one was looking at her nails. Phillip had gone back to Washington the day after his party, as promised, and they'd conversed a few times via email. He'd called twice to say hi, but so far, they hadn't connected for dinner. She wasn't upset. He'd let her know when he was free and that obviously hadn't happened yet.

It was exactly what she'd signed up for. A night of passion with an amazing man who paid attention to her. She still dreamed about the way his mouth felt on hers and how gorgeous that man's body was. Sure, she'd have liked to see him again, but that might mean having a conversation about what dating meant for them and she didn't want to ruin the magic with real-life fears and hang-ups.

If the test came back positive, they'd be having a hell of a conversation about dates, that was for sure. Due dates, birth dates, playdates. It was mind-boggling.

She peered into the toilet. Nothing. Or maybe something. Did the results window look a little pink? Her stomach flipped over and back again. "What do the instructions say about how to read this test? What does it mean if it's pink?"

She'd read them herself but panic drove the information from her brain.

"One pink line is not pregnant. Two pink lines is pregnant. You've *never* taken a pregnancy test before?" Cass didn't bother to keep the incredulity from her tone. "Not even in college?"

"No," Alex muttered. "You'd have to have sex to need one."

She'd been just as awkward and clumsy in college as she was now. Men shied away, for the most part. Phillip was a rare exception.

Please, God, do not let that exception have irreversible consequences.

More pink bled into the window. A distinct line appeared. *One* line. That meant not pregnant. Except the pink was still wicking through the window, spreading its impersonal message about huge, life-alerting events.

"Why are you making me do this?"

"Because you clearly weren't ever going to do it yourself. It's been four weeks since Phillip's party," Cass reminded her, as if she needed reminding. "If you are pregnant, you're a third of the way through the first trimester. Denial is not a good health-care plan for you or a baby."

Baby. Oh, God. Alex had staunchly refused to even think that word. And then…a second line appeared in the window, pink and vivid and final.

"Hand me the second test," Alex demanded hoarsely. She'd wondered why they'd included two. Obviously so people in her position could make absolutely sure.

Cass did so without comment and they waited in silence for the second confirmation.

"How accurate are these things?" Alex whispered, as again, two pink lines materialized in the window.

"Pretty accurate," Cass confirmed. "Sometimes it says you're not pregnant when you really are because you've taken the test too early. But if it says you *are* pregnant, that's like 100 percent. I'm guessing it was positive. Both times."

And now it was a reality, an undeniable, unfixable reality.

Alex was pregnant with Senator Phillip Edgewood's baby.

Flipping the latch to unlock the wide door, she stumbled from the bathroom stall—how, she didn't know, when everything was numb. Except her mind, of course. That was on full speed in a Tilt-a-Whirl of thoughts, none of which were cohesive.

She was going to be a mom. A life was growing inside her through the miracle of procreation. It hardly seemed possible.

Cass took one look at Alex's face and engulfed her in a hug, holding her tight as if the sheer pressure might keep Alex together. "It'll be okay."

"How?" Alex mumbled into Cass's shoulder. "How will it be okay?"

She was going to be a *mom*. The idea terrified her. Deep inside, she knew she could do it. She had her own mom to fall back on and look to for guidance. Alex was smart—present circumstances excluded. She had her own money and house. Maybe it *would* be okay.

Phillip. She had to go see him. For one brief, bright second she envisioned him opening the door, seeing her and breaking into a wide smile that she'd feel all the way to her toes. He'd confess he'd missed her, had been thinking about her and was glad she'd come by. She'd smile back and something meaningful would pass between them. She'd admit she'd thought about him, too. That she wished he'd called even though she knew why he hadn't.

And then she'd tell him he was going to be a father. She had no idea how he'd react. Because she didn't really know him at all.

"It's a mess." Alex pulled from Cass's embrace.

"It's a wonderful, joyous event to be celebrated amongst friends," Cass corrected brightly. "You're the first of us to get pregnant. Harper and Trinity will be thrilled."

"About what?" Harper asked as the two women in question joined Alex's nightmare right on cue. Fyra's chief science officer's red hair was down today, framing Harper's lovely face, and she'd got it cut, but Alex was too shell-shocked to comment on it.

Trinity's keen gaze zigzagged between Cass and Alex as she crossed her arms over a chic suit in a vivid shade of blue that matched the stripe coloring the right side of her dark hair. "Something's going on. Did something happen on the FDA approval front? What did Phillip say?"

His name was like a knife through Alex's heart, especially since she hadn't thought about Formula-47's FDA application one time over the past week. That was what she should have been focusing on, not her stupid crush on the man helping Fyra with the approval process.

This was the absolute worst timing. Fyra was poised to hit the billion-dollars-a-year mark in revenue with Harper's revolutionary new skin-care formula, and Alex couldn't do a simple thing like working with the senator on the FDA approval process without messing it all up.

"Phillip didn't call," she told Trinity, who she knew was chomping at the bit to get started on a new marketing campaign. "I'm pregnant."

Harper and Trinity exclaimed happily and took turns hugging her. She had her friends, if nothing else. She breathed easier.

Cass smiled and rubbed her back. "See? We'll hold your hand through it and be your village. Single women raise children all the time."

Single mom. Oh, God. She hadn't even got that far in her mind. It wasn't just a pregnancy, but a child who needed nurturing and love.

The complexities nearly knocked her knees out from under her. She'd never intended to have children, never planned to expose a helpless child to pain and suffering at the hands of adults. Her own parents' divorce had changed her, hardened her, driven her into teenage experimentation with drugs and alcohol, then ultimately a brush with the law. And now she'd done the one thing she'd sworn to never do—force a child to live with his or her parents' mistakes.

This was what happened when she threw caution to the wind.

Cass had made a broad, sweeping assumption that Alex would be handling this without Phillip, but nothing could be further from what Alex had envisioned. Babies needed a family. A father. She hadn't had one and knew that pain. Her child would have one come hell or high water.

Did Phillip even want kids? What if he would be happier washing his hands of her and the baby, perfectly fine with never seeing either of them again? How would she convince him otherwise if he hated the idea of being a dad?

And what kind of relationship would she and Phillip have? How could they be parents when they weren't even a couple? Panic sloshed through her already nauseated stomach.

"When did you become an expert on motherhood?" Alex snapped, too freaked to temper her tone.

"Since Gage got full custody of Robbie," Cass said simply. "Just because I didn't give birth to him doesn't make him any less mine. I wanted to learn."

Cass had fallen in love with a single father and thus had to become a mother in short order. Looked like Alex would be doing the same.

A horrifying thought occurred to her then.

Maybe Phillip *would* want to raise the baby...without her. Oh, God. What if he tried to use his power and influence to take the baby away for some reason? Instantly, she cradled her still-flat stomach protectively. He wouldn't do that. Would he? She bemoaned the fact that she didn't know him well enough to guess.

It didn't matter. No one was taking this baby from her. The child was equally hers and Phillip's, and they were both going to have a role in its life. Period.

No child of hers was going to grow up without a loving mother *and* father. That started by talking to Phillip about how they would manage the next eighteen-plus years together and ended with honesty. She certainly didn't need his money, but what she did need from him would require courage and fortitude to secure.

"I have to see a doctor. To confirm. And then fly to Washington," she told Cass woodenly. "I know it's the worst time to be gone, but—"

"Don't be ridiculous. Go. Take the time you need to figure out the next steps. We'll be here."

Yes. Next steps. If she took this in the logical order everything would be fine.

Trinity and Harper both nodded, throwing in their own versions of support and talking a mile a minute about nursery decor, breast-feeding and maternity fashion.

"Thanks." Alex's throat closed and she couldn't say anything else. Just as well. She needed to save her voice for the long conversation with Phillip looming in her future.

Phillip typed his electronic signature and sent the email. One thing off his growing list.

Cherry trees outside his office window had burst into full bloom in the past week. Spring was Phillip's favorite time in Washington, though he enjoyed the snowy winter, too. Winter in Dallas consisted of ice storms followed by seventy-degree days. The ups and downs were maddening.

He wished his grandfather agreed. The man had spent years and years living in DC while he'd held office, but as his health declined, Max Edgewood preferred to stay in Dallas. It was the one reason Phillip commuted back and forth as much as he did; he loved his grandfather and gladly split his time between the two cities. He didn't like to think about how few days Max might have left on this earth.

In fact, they were overdue for a visit. He should go home soon. Except he was avoiding Dallas.

Linda buzzed him through the phone intercom. "Senator, Ms. Meer is here."

A myriad of emotions flushed through his body at the mention of the woman he'd fled to Washington to forget.

He'd failed spectacularly at the forgetting part, but he'd been trying to at least stay away. No matter how much he'd wanted to arrange that dinner they'd discussed, they were all wrong for each other and she'd given him the perfect out by telling him to call when he was free. If he was at the Capitol, he wasn't free.

What was Alex doing in Washington? It was almost as if she'd known he couldn't stop thinking about their night together. Or, more realistically, she was here about the FDA approval process. They *were* still working together.

This wasn't the first time she'd stopped by his office. It was, however, the first time she'd come by without an appointment. It was a testament to his admin's superior mind-reading skills that she hadn't turned Alex away.

"Send her in immediately," he told Linda.

He stood as the door opened and Alex spilled into the room. Gone were the makeup and fancy clothes, replaced by her typical ponytail and jeans.

Her bare face glowed and something seized his lungs as he stared at her. She was even more beautiful without all the trappings she'd worn to his party. Breathtaking almost, as if something inside her had suddenly become illuminated.

"Hi," he greeted her inanely after a long moment of silence.

She'd stolen his ability to think simply by walking into the room. That was not supposed to happen. He'd expressly promised things wouldn't be weird between them once he knew what she looked like under that formfitting T-shirt... and he was making it weird.

"Hi," she repeated and shifted uncomfortably. "Thanks for seeing me on short notice. I'm sorry to barge in here without calling first."

"I'm glad." He smiled, feeling a bit more on even ground. "I'm happy to see you."

"You might not feel that way in a minute."

Her eyes shone with unexpected moisture and he lost his place again. This wasn't a social visit, obviously. "Is something wrong?"

"Maybe." She hesitated, biting her lip in that way that said she didn't know what to say next. "You didn't ever issue that dinner invitation."

Not here to talk business, then. The uncertainty glinting in her eyes put a cramp in his stomach.

"I'm sorry," he said sincerely and cursed himself for being such an ass. "I could give you a bunch of excuses, but none of them would be the truth. I didn't think it was fair to you to continue our relationship. So I didn't."

But he'd dreamed of things happening differently. A lot. If only he could take her in his arms and kiss her hello, like he wanted to.

"Because you got what you were after and now you're done?" she whispered.

The simple question whacked him between the eyes. He'd hurt her feelings with his stupid rules and the loneliness that had caused him to act selfishly.

"That's not it at all." True, and yet nowhere near the whole truth. He *was* done, but not for the reasons she seemed to think. He sighed. "I like you a lot, Alex, but I'm not sure we're meant to continue our affair. It's complicated. And not your fault. I wish things could be different. And not so complicated."

She choked out a laugh that sounded a bit like a sob. "Yeah, I wish that, too. Unfortunately, things are far more complicated than you could ever dream."

"What—"

"I'm pregnant."

His expression froze into place, a practiced mechanism to keep his audience from guessing his thoughts before he was ready to share them.

Pregnant.

The simple word bled through his mind and fractured into pieces as a thousand simultaneous thoughts vied for attention. *Pregnant.* It echoed, tearing through his heart painfully. The obvious question—whether she thought he was the father—clearly didn't need to be asked. She wouldn't be here otherwise.

Now would be a good time to say something. "That's an unexpected development."

Because he needed to do something with his hands, he pushed the intercom button. "Linda, can you bring Ms. Meer a bottle of water?"

Then he rounded the three-hundred-year-old desk that had been his grandfather's, gifted to Phillip when his grand-father retired, and hustled Alex to the couch where he some-times slept when he couldn't face his lonely condo on 2nd Street. "Please. Sit down."

She complied, sinking to the couch as if her bones couldn't hold her upright any longer. He knew the feeling. Linda hur-ried in with the water and handed it to Alex with a friendly nod and then disappeared, as a good admin should.

"I'm sorry to blurt it out like that," Alex said solemnly and drank the water. "I don't phrase things well under the best circumstances and I'm still kind of in shock."

"I would imagine so." Blearily, he scrubbed his face with his hands and breathed deeply. For fortitude. It didn't help. "How do you feel? Okay? Do you need a paper bag? I'll get you one as long as you share it with me."

She flashed a brief smile. "Are you having sympathy morning sickness?"

"No, I was thinking about breathing into it." Because he felt like he might pass out. "It's my baby, right?"

"Yeah." Her smile disappeared. "I'm not all that good at luring men into bed. Look how long it took for me to get you there. But we can do a paternity test while I'm here, if you want."

The sooner, the better. He trusted Alex, but he couldn't afford mistakes.

This could *not* be happening. Phillip had lived his life carefully for nearly two decades. Even as a teenager, he'd been mindful that political aspirations could die easily with the wrong decisions, and he'd never had a reason to conceal his actions. While other politicians paid off former mistresses and employed spin doctors to get them out of hot water with the media, Phillip preferred honesty— after all, if you never did anything questionable, you didn't have to cover it up.

This was all his fault. The condoms must have been older than he'd remembered. And now they'd both pay the price.

Pregnant. Alex was pregnant.

He couldn't repeat it enough times for it to stick in his brain as a fact, like the way he knew the sky was blue without looking at it. Alex was a great person, a businesswoman he was helping navigate the bureaucracy of the FDA approval process. Thinking of her like that was easy. She was also a sexy woman whose company he'd enjoyed at a party a few weeks ago.

And now she had a third designation: the mother of his child.

It changed everything.

They had to get married. His heart squeezed painfully once, and he shut it down ruthlessly. There was so much more to consider here than how he'd always thought he'd have a baby with Gina. So much more to consider than Alex's lack of credentials as the perfect wife to fit his needs.

If he planned to be honest with his constituents, there was no other solution than to surround Alex, his child and his career with the protection of marriage. No man with Phillip's political platform could ascend to the Oval Office with an illegitimate child any sooner than he could as a single man. The press would eat him alive, gleefully portraying his family values as hypocrisy.

Except all he could think about was Alex spread out on his bed, underneath him, as he made love to her. What would it be like to wake up to her in the morning? He couldn't lie to himself any more than he could to his supporters; marrying her meant they could continue that part of their relationship.

The pregnancy meant he could have Alex and keep his emotional commitment to Gina, because of course Alex wouldn't expect him to be in love with her. He could raise his baby with his child's mother. The rest of the complications were a huge compromise, but one he was willing to make for the benefits.

He had no clue whether Alex would marry him under those conditions, but he had to try to convince her.

She cleared her throat. "We need to talk about next steps."

"Agreed." His mind raced through his calendar, rearranging appointments and projects. He could carve out time for the flurry of activity that was about to become both their realities. He had to. "My mother will want to plan a huge splashy ceremony, but I can probably talk her off the ledge if you'd rather have something a bit simpler."

His parents would be thrilled he'd finally moved on. His mom had bemoaned never having grandkids twice a week for over a year, and at least this development would make her happy.

She stared at him. "Your mother will want to have a ceremony to announce the pregnancy? Don't take this the wrong way, but that's very strange."

Flubbed that up, moron.

When he'd asked Gina to marry him he'd gone the distance with a surprise trip to Venice, a hired violinist and a ten-carat diamond that had once belonged to a Vanderbilt. But he'd had considerably longer than ten minutes to plan it and a huge gaping hole in his life that only Gina could fill.

Yet he was about to start a family with Alex instead. Yes, he liked her, but the biggest decision he'd thought he had in relation to her was whether he'd break his promise to himself about not calling her. It was numbing how quickly everything had turned on its head.

This woman was going to be his wife if he had anything to say about it. He needed to start acting like it.

"I'm sorry. Let's back up." He took her hand and held it, though why he thought that small bit of contact would help, he couldn't say. "Alex, we have to get married."

And that wasn't much better as proposals went.

Her face went white and she snatched her hand away from his as if he'd scalded her. "Married? Why would we get married? That's insane. We don't know each other."

The note of desperation in her voice didn't sit well. "We don't know each other well enough to be parents either, but facts are facts. As the baby's father, I want to consider what's best for him or her. Unless the paternity-test results might offer another reason for your denial?"

Something broke open inside him as he thought about Alex with another man. Irrational, to be sure, especially since he was the one who hadn't called. He didn't own her.

But he had never stopped thinking about her, or her sweet fire as they'd connected—her skin, her eyes, all of it. He wouldn't apologize for having a strong attraction to a woman who'd just announced she was carrying his child, nor for the fact that marriage meant he was the only one allowed the privilege of sleeping with her. Fidelity was as much a part of his makeup as statesmanship. There was no denying that she still affected him, and if they were living together, it was a natural conclusion that they'd continue their physical relationship. He certainly wanted to.

"No, of course not," she said. "This is your baby."

In DC, the first thing you learned was how to tell if someone was lying. She wasn't. Regardless, he needed to make sure. The test could be done relatively quickly and would only confirm what he already knew in his gut.

"Here's what we're going to do." The plan rolled through his head. "I'll clear my schedule for the day and we'll get the test. Then will you agree to talk about what comes next?"

Hesitating, she blinked and met his gaze, vulnerability and fear in her expression. It prompted him to fix whatever was wrong so she'd smile again. He ached to take her into his arms. For comfort, not to kiss her, though he'd have sworn a minute ago that sparks were the only thing between them.

Even that was too much.

The way Alex affected him clashed with the place inside that belonged to his first wife. That unsettled him nearly as much as the idea of Alex being pregnant. But if he wanted to have a family—and he did—not only would he have to convince Alex marriage was the best option, he would have to convince himself to stay strong against the tide of emotions she elicited.

No second chances in life or love. That meant he would never have feelings for another woman. This compromise might be harder than he'd envisioned.

"Okay," she said, her voice low. "We can talk. But you'll

have to rethink the idea of marriage. I'm not a member of the cult of love and romance."

She wasn't? He stared at her as his argument for marriage shifted gears and fell into place.

Four

The results of the paternity test didn't take long. With Phillip's connections, he had paperwork in his hand before lunch proving the baby Alex carried was 100 percent his.

Like she'd told him. It stung a little to hear him question her, as if Alex might have tried to pass off another man's baby as his. Who *did* something like that?

Okay, it stung a lot. But she tried not to fume about it as Phillip's driver navigated the enormous limousine through Washington, DC, traffic. Her baby's father sat next to her on the long bench seat, still clutching the results from the private physician's office they'd visited to perform the test.

"Are you hungry?" Phillip asked, his tone polite but distant, as it had been since the moment she'd uttered the word *pregnant*.

She secretly called it his Senator Mask, and she'd noted he pulled it on when the circumstances dictated he be tolerant and friendly without inviting too much familiarity.

He'd put on the mask in meetings and at the party a couple of times but always toward others. She'd never thought he'd direct it at her.

"I don't think I could eat, no," she murmured. Her stomach wasn't in any condition to accept food and not just because of the morning sickness that should be renamed *24/7 sickness*. "But if you want to find a quiet restaurant where we can talk, you're welcome to eat. I wouldn't mind a cup of hot tea."

It was time to make some decisions. Unfortunately, she feared neither of them liked the choices all that well. And she had a feeling the subject of marriage was about to come up again.

Alex and Phillip were not getting married under any circumstances. Marriage was for other people, foolish people who believed love could last forever. Who believed in happily-ever-after. There was nothing he could say to convince her. Besides, marriage didn't make any sense.

"Maybe we should drive around. This car is about as private as it gets." Flashing her a distracted smile, Phillip hit the intercom to speak to the driver. "Randy, would you mind stopping at the next Starbucks and purchasing Ms. Meer a cup of hot tea?"

Something squished in her chest. The man never missed a trick. Alex found herself returning his smile even though his wasn't the genuine one she preferred. How was it possible that pregnancy could drive such a wedge between them? They were still the same people as the night of the party. They'd shared jokes and laughed, and he'd looked at her like she was the only person in the room he cared about.

Since that type of attention had got her in this situation, maybe it was better that he wasn't flirting with her. She missed it, though.

Phillip's driver whipped into a parking lot, and with the efficiency she'd come to expect from Phillip's staff, he handed her a white to-go cup before she'd barely registered that he'd stopped. She nodded her thanks.

Hot tea in hand, she stared out the window at the bustling city her baby's father called home for much of the year. Might as well jump right into it. "Before you start talking about marriage again, just know that I can't even consider it. Marriage doesn't work under the best of circumstances, let alone the worst."

He contemplated her as he pulled a water bottle from a hidden compartment on his left side. Did the lavishness at Phillip's disposal ever end? Alex made a healthy salary, but she rarely spent money on more than necessities. Phillip came from old oil money and his wealth far eclipsed hers. The imbalance had never seemed all that important before, but in the face of making decisions about things like custody, lifestyles, nannies and public schools versus private, the gulf between them widened.

"As long as we're sharing philosophies," Phillip said, "let me tell you something about mine."

He wasn't looking at the traffic. His focus was solely on her and it tripped her pulse.

"Sure."

"I can't remember a time when I wasn't aware that my family had something unique about it. Adults in my world discussed important issues at the dinner table. We went to rallies and talked to farmers, industrial workers, bankers and moms during cross-country trips. I was fascinated by the activity. I learned more about the daily life and burdens of the average American before the age of ten than most people are probably ever aware of."

"You were born into a political dynasty, Phillip," she interjected in the pause. "I get that."

He nodded. "You met my father, the congressman. My grandfather was a senator and so was my uncle. It's in our blood to care about making things better for our country."

Oddly enough, the more Phillip talked about his job, the more quickly his Senator Mask faded. It was a little breathtaking to watch him morph back into the man who had so charmed her from their first meeting and nearly every second since then.

She didn't dare interrupt. This was the Phillip she'd dreamed about. The one she'd gladly donned makeup and a dress to get closer to. Her pregnancy didn't erase his magnetic appeal in the slightest.

"So now I'm going to have a son or daughter," he continued. "I always envisioned my kids having a similar childhood to the one that solidified my path."

That implied he planned to have more kids. That sounded nice—for *him*—but she wasn't concerned about children that didn't exist yet. Only the one that did. "I'm sorry, but—"

"Wait." He shushed her gently. "I'm getting to the important part. I married Gina with my heart and eyes wideopen. We were going to have that life I just described and then she was gone. It was a single-car accident and no one could say for sure what had happened other than a telephone pole in the wrong place. The devastation… I can't go through that again. So I'm not a fan of marriage, either. At least not the kind of marriage I had with her."

"There's another kind?" Alex blurted out before she thought better of it.

She'd been caught up in watching his face as he talked about his first wife. The emotions were heartbreaking. What would it be like to be married to a man who loved you that much? Up until this moment, she hadn't realized it was possible to love someone so much that even the distance of two years wouldn't fully dull the pain of losing them.

Obviously Phillip was the exception to the rule that love didn't last.

"There are all kinds of marriages," Phillip said. "That's why you can't say for sure that no marriages work."

Was that where he was going with this? "Sure I can. I didn't have a fairy-tale childhood like yours. I lived through a really bad divorce and it doesn't matter what kind of marriage my parents had because the ultimate result was that it ended. Just like yours did. That's why marriages don't work, because when they end, people get hurt. That's why a marriage between *us* wouldn't work."

"Not if we do it differently," he suggested calmly, despite her rising agitation. "Hear me out."

Genuine curiosity got the better of her. If he'd spouted romantic poetry or autocratic demands, she'd order him to stop the car. But logic? The man couldn't have picked a better way to get her attention. "Okay. I'll bite. What kind of marriage could we possibly have that would work, Phillip?"

"One based on partnership. We're about to become parents. I'd like to raise our child together, without shuttling him or her between us. I want us to be on the same page about things like discipline. I want to celebrate holidays together. Share milestones. I think that's best accomplished by being a unit."

His deep voice slid along her skin as he wove a picture with words. A picture that dug into the core of her hurt and disappointment about her parents' divorce and promised that her child wouldn't have to endure what she had.

It was fool's gold, though. All the things he talked about depended on their commitment to each other never dying. It depended on no one changing their mind at some point down the road and ripping out the heart of the family that they'd built.

"But we don't have to be married to make parenting decisions together," she said. "And if we're not married, we never have to go through a divorce."

No marriage meant no one got hurt. No child of hers would ever have to be the product of a broken home.

But the line she'd just drawn might also mean her child wouldn't get to know his or her father, not like she'd envisioned. She couldn't have it both ways.

If she and Phillip didn't live in the same house, how would Christmas morning work? They'd have to split custody and explain that Santa came to two houses for some children. But she would always feel that something wasn't quite right. And the arrangements might mean that some years, she wouldn't even have her child with her on Christmas morning. Or a random Tuesday when her child took his or her first steps. The first day of school, learning to ride a bike—the list went on and on.

There were thousands of things she might miss if she and Phillip set up a custody agreement. Things he would miss. The baby was half his, no matter what, and she wanted her baby to have a father. A *present* father, not one that swooped in on weekends.

Panic fluttered her pulse. How in the world had she got here?

"Or…" He reached out then and captured her hand, threading his fingers through hers. "We have a marriage with no expectations other than divorce isn't an option."

No expectations.

It was an intentional echo of their singular night together, when passion had been the only thing that mattered.

Her gaze flew to his, caught and held. His blue eyes were mesmerizing as he tilted his head slightly and let that smile she loved spill over his face. Breath tangled in her lungs as he brushed her thumb with his.

"Tell me what a marriage with no expectations looks like," she murmured because her throat had gone completely dry.

"It means we take love out of the equation. That's what causes all the hurt. The loss of it is what drives people to end things. If we start out as friends and partners with no expectations of anything more, we can have the kind of marriage that lasts. Then divorce doesn't even come up."

The logic flowed over Alex like a balm. She'd never understood the hoopla over moonlight and candles, but Phillip had figured out how to romance her with reason. It was extremely affecting.

"I like you," Phillip continued, his smile deepening. "And I think you like me. We're obviously a match in the bedroom, which not even couples in love can always say. If we establish some ground rules from the beginning, no one gets hurt. We're just two people raising a child and living our lives together."

Rules for marriage. How…safe. And clear. She did like rules.

Never in a million years had she imagined he'd find a way to get her to consider this insane idea. But here she was…thinking about matrimony. His point made a brilliant sort of sense. Her baby would have a father. She'd never have to miss a thing.

Somehow, she'd found a man who didn't have one single emotional demand. She'd have someone by her side to help raise the baby, and they'd have a deal up front to stay together. No one was making any promises they couldn't keep.

"So no expectations." She rolled it around in her head.

"You don't care if we never fall in love? Because I don't even know if I have that capacity. Nor the desire."

Since she'd never even come close to feeling giggly and romantic about a man, she'd always assumed she didn't have the right temperament for it.

He was quiet for a moment. "It's not that I don't care. It's that I don't want to be in love with anyone other than Gina. Most women wouldn't put up with that in a marriage. Fortunately for me, you're not most women."

It should have been the final argument that won her over. She'd never have to question whether love would become a factor in their relationship because his heart wasn't available. But something wasn't adding up here.

"Just out of curiosity, why marriage, then? Why don't we just live together?"

"Simple." He shrugged. "I don't want to. It serves many purposes to marry you. I'm a senator. Marriage is something my constituents would expect. I believe in family values, which will be a central part of my platform when I run for president."

"President? Of the United States?" Her voice might have gone up a full octave but she couldn't tell for sure around the sudden rush of blood from her head. "When were you going to tell me that part?"

She couldn't be the First Lady. She didn't have the flair for it. Or the ability to talk to the press. She'd rather eat bugs than have that kind of attention dogging her for the rest of her life.

"I'm telling you now," he said calmly and squeezed her hand. "Because that's an important part of this discussion. I'm running for president within the next few years and it would greatly benefit my campaign if I was married. My child is going to be in the spotlight no matter what. My child's mother is going to be a subject of interest. If you'd like to weather that on your own, I can't decide that for you. But marriage affords you a measure of protection, especially as I'm campaigning and definitely if I win."

More logic. And it made a certain sort of sense. Enough to deepen her panic. "I can't be a politician's wife! I can barely talk to you, let alone the press."

There would be no hiding behind a statue for the rest of her life if she married Phillip. Her stomach turned over as the limo made another loop around the Washington Monument.

"I have people who can help with that, Alex. Stylists. Speech writers." He cupped her chin, and his fingers on her face soothed her as she stared at his earnest expression. "I like you the way you are, but if it would make you more comfortable to have more polish as you stand by my side at a press conference, okay. I'll help you with that."

Mute, she stared at him. No expectation for Alex to morph into the perfect politician's wife, either? Part of her was grateful and wanted to respond to such grace positively. Of course she'd try not to embarrass him. Why wouldn't she?

The other part of her was a bit suspicious. "I don't have to dress up if I don't feel like it?"

"The only thing you need to worry about is whether you want to do this with me. Whether you want our child to have the life I've been describing."

Oh, no, there was so much more to consider. Speaking of which, would she have to live in Washington if they got married? What about her career? "What about my company? I have a job. I can't walk off and leave it."

Fyra was everything to her. Surely he wasn't saying she needed to give it up. Not only did she owe Cass for giving her a chance, she loved her job.

"That could be a challenge. I won't lie. But we'll figure something out. We have to," he said.

"It's not the life either of us imagined," he continued. "It's not going to be easy. But it will be worth it for our baby and for us personally. We'll be doing it together. As partners operating under an up-front agreement but also as friends. Like we've been all along."

His smooth voice drew her in, convincing her. She might have to do some things she didn't like, but the rewards for their child would outweigh her discomfort.

And there were other potential benefits she couldn't help but wonder about.

"What about sharing a bedroom?" she murmured, and the temperature in the close confines of the limo shot up instantly as they watched each other, the question hanging between them.

"Ah, now, that's the part of this discussion I was waiting for." He tilted his head a touch closer. Almost within kissing distance. "I'm in favor of whatever you decide. But I would have a very difficult time keeping my hands off you behind closed doors. Even if we didn't share a bedroom."

"Really?" That hummed through her pleasantly. Did Phillip find her that attractive? There was something delicious about being wanted, especially by a man like Phillip. He'd rocked her with his careful attention, both in and out of bed. Imagine if that continued.

"Oh, are you confused about that?"

Without warning, he pulled her forward, almost hauling her into his lap. His mouth hit hers in a searing kiss that spoke of his desire far more clearly than words ever could.

The promise bled through his fingers, into her skin, heating her as she fell into this kiss. As her senses exploded with Phillip. He kissed her masterfully, purposefully.

When he pulled back, she nearly wept.

"I'd like an intimate marriage in every sense of the word," he rasped, clearly as affected as she was.

She'd wished for something to fill the void in her life—perhaps she'd found it. She just couldn't help but think she'd bitten off more than she could chew.

"With the exception of love," she reminded him. Just to reiterate the ground rules.

"Right. I had that once and I'm not a believer in second chances."

That was a hard line to take. Second chances were sometimes the only thing standing between a person and the rest of her life. Without a second chance, Alex wouldn't have been afforded the opportunity to start over after nearly ruining her life.

What if he didn't like the fact that she'd needed a second chance? That had to be hashed out now, not later.

Nodding once, she took a deep breath. "Then there's something you need to know before you make a final decision about marrying me. You could find this out for yourself with your connections. But I want you to hear it from me. When I was fifteen, I was arrested and convicted of theft. I got probation and my record was sealed. But the media might find a way to dig it up if my husband is running for president. I thought you should know."

Phillip's expression didn't change. "Is that the extent of your record?"

"Yes." Because it was the only crime she'd got caught doing. Not because it was the only illegal thing she'd ever done.

"I'll get my publicist on it immediately. If we talk about it up front, we can play it off as youthful indiscretion. This is exactly why marriage is important for you, too. If I can forgive it, the world can, too."

He made all of this sound too easy. She had a feeling

he'd knock down any argument she threw out because he'd decided what he wanted and planned to wear her down until she accepted the inevitable. "I never really had a choice about marrying you, did I?"

He flashed a grin. "Of course you do. Would you like some time to think about it?"

No, they could debate this to death or get started on the rest of their lives. "Where do I sign?"

That got a genuine laugh out of him. "We can let our lawyers handle that. In the meantime, we have a wedding to plan."

The idea exhausted her. Other women must love that kind of thing, but a wedding? How fancy did it have to be? Maybe they could elope. "I'd rather eat some toast and take a nap. Don't you have people who can handle a wedding?"

His eyes glowed as he smiled. "Absolutely, if that's your preference. Let me take care of everything. You pick out a dress and show up."

That sounded so nice. No picking out floral arrangements and visiting venues for the reception? Senator Edgewood had her vote. He really was making this easy on her.

She had a feeling that might not last. Especially since she had a suspicion he'd glossed over every single one of her objections for a yet-to-be-established reason. He needed her. Why remained to be seen.

Music rang out in the sanctuary, signaling the start of the ceremony. Phillip trained his eyes on the double doors at the rear of the Methodist church north of downtown Dallas where his parents had been members for thirty years. He hadn't seen Alex in over a week and for some odd reason it had put a hitch in his stride.

This wedding served a purpose. It wasn't supposed to be sentimental. Or emotional. It was a compromise. He and Alex had a deal to be partners in raising their child and they'd agreed it made sense to be legally married. She was okay with the fact that he wanted to stay loyal to his love for Gina. He was okay with her lack of social skills.

Nerves shouldn't be a factor. But as he waited for his bride to make an appearance, he couldn't call this jumpiness under his skin anything but nerves.

In the next few moments, Alexandra Meer would officially become Mrs. Edgewood. Not only was she about to become his wife, in less than seven months they'd be parents. It was mind-boggling.

The doors burst open and the first woman in lilac solemnly paraded toward him. Dr. Harper Livingston, the genius scientist behind Formula-47, the product for which Alex's company needed FDA approval, was followed by a second woman in lilac. Trinity Forrester, Fyra's chief marketing officer, cut quite a figure with her angular black hair and stilettos. CEO Cassandra Claremont glided down the aisle next, her gaze fastened firmly on the man to Phillip's right, her fiancé, Gage Branson. Gage had been the only person Phillip would have asked to be his best man, considering his cousin was the one who had introduced him to Alex.

In a marriage based on appearances, no detail was too small.

And then Alex walked into the room and his heart thumped once, then paused for the longest, strangest skipped beat.

Alex had selected white for the occasion, but the minimalist design allowed the woman to shine through. Phillip couldn't tear his gaze from her beautiful face, which had the lightest smattering of color in deference to the photographs that would be taken later. The uncharacteristic makeup only enhanced the natural beauty of the woman he had somehow convinced to marry him.

He still didn't know what had tipped the scales. Still hadn't fully taken a deep breath until this moment, because what if she changed her mind? He refused to consider any of this an emotional investment. He needed a wife, and it would be twice as difficult to find one willing to step into a marriage of convenience after the press finished crucifying him over his purported family values while his illegitimate child lived with a single mom.

Five hundred guests, ranging from the United States secretary of state, to a French hotel magnate, to Alex's mom, watched as Alex floated down the aisle toward him. She reached his side and he took her hand. She was trembling.

"You okay?" he whispered as the minister started the dearly-beloveds. Instantly, all thoughts of plans and campaigns and ground rules vanished as he focused on Alex.

"No." All the color leached out of her face, which became a remarkable match for her dress. "Will you be really mad at me if I throw up on that suit?"

Morning sickness was taking a huge toll on her, which was part of the reason they hadn't seen each other—she'd been too ill to fly and he'd had to burn the midnight oil in Washington in order to take off a few days for the wedding.

"Well, it's not what I'd envisioned for our vows," he acknowledged wryly. "But perhaps appropriate under the circumstances."

"Don't make me laugh," she muttered as a smile tugged at her mouth. "I'm trying to keep down the four bites of toast I had for breakfast. Remind me again why we couldn't elope?"

The minister launched into a series of lines that Phillip's mother had painstakingly selected after being given the job. Their immediate family and close friends knew Alex was pregnant, but they'd kept it secret otherwise. At only ten weeks, she wasn't showing yet, so there was no reason to eclipse the wedding with baby news.

"Because," Phillip said out of the side of his mouth. "Pomp and circumstance are part of the deal."

She moaned. "I don't see how it's fair that I have to both carry the baby and smile at guests."

"I'll tell you what. After the birth, I'll carry the baby. How's that for fair?"

The minister cleared his throat. Phillip glanced back at the man, having completely lost track of the ceremony. "I do."

Nodding, the minister repeated the questions to Alex, who also said, "I do," and after sliding their respective rings on each other's third fingers, it was done. They were married with none of the emotion of the first time he'd done this.

It was a relief. Alex had distracted him from thinking about Gina from the moment she'd appeared, and he was oddly grateful for her good humor in the face of not feeling well. He'd thought this day would be difficult to get through, but Alex had turned that on its head by holding a conversation during the ceremony.

No expectations. It was a strange mantra for marriage, but for an unconventional agreement like theirs, it worked. So far.

"Is it okay if I kiss you?" Phillip whispered in case she didn't want anyone else to know her stomach was upset.

She scowled. "Of course. It would seem weird if you didn't."

But then it was weird anyway because five hundred people were watching. Would they know this marriage wasn't a loving union? That was one aspect he and Alex hadn't discussed—if they were going to act like a traditional married couple in front of others.

Since there was no time to chat about it, he turned her away from the crowd so they had a measure of privacy.

When he cupped her face, she smiled and it filled him from the inside out. Suddenly, it didn't matter who was watching. He kissed her and she opened underneath his mouth. For a moment, he soaked in the perfection of how this woman he'd just married fit against him.

He hugged her deeper into his embrace and let the one part of himself that wasn't off-limits to her have free rein. His body reacted like it always did whenever Alex got within a few feet. Which wasn't necessarily appropriate for a crowded church, any more so than it had been for a crowded party. There was no giant statue here, so he reluctantly let her go to the sound of applause and swelling music.

Breathlessly, she regained her balance, her lips red and bare of lipstick. Funny, he'd got to the point where he preferred her without makeup now that he had a basis for comparison.

Phillip took his bride's hand and they walked down the aisle together as husband and wife. With the wedding out of the way, it was all downhill from here.

Five

Phillip couldn't concentrate on the guests he'd invited to the reception.

Alex had invited some friends and family but the majority of the guest list consisted of movers and shakers from around the globe: people who benefited his future campaign for the White House. People he owed favors to for previous campaigns. People he knew from Congress. Old friends of his parents, who happened to own most of Dallas. Every one of the attendees on his guest list had significant power and influence.

This wedding wasn't a joyous celebration of the union between two lovers, like the one he'd shared with Gina, but a carefully orchestrated event designed for a future presidential campaign. He had to think about it that way, or he wouldn't get through it. Or at least that had been the plan.

But instead, all Phillip could think about was his new wife, who had fled to the bathroom almost thirty minutes ago. She'd been trailed by three women in lilac, so he knew she was in good hands. But not *one* of them could be bothered to take two minutes and bring him word that Alex was okay?

He was worried about her. The baby was half his and he couldn't carry it, but he could at least be there to help ease Alex's discomfort. Get her water or *something*. Why hadn't she asked for him?

Senator Galindo breezed by with her husband, the CEO of a telecommunications company. They chatted for a moment and then Alex joined their group, a small smile in place.

Finally, he could assess her condition for himself. Make sure she didn't need to go home and lie down. She looked so uncomfortable that his heart twisted. He hated that she felt this awful at what was supposed to be their debut as a couple.

Not much point in marrying a wife to stand by his side who wasn't able to, or at least that was what he tried to tell himself. Sternly. But he didn't care about the loss of his plus one at a key networking event when his wife's face was tinted a hue best suited for frogs.

"Alex, I don't think you've met Senator Ramona Galindo." Phillip forced himself through the niceties of introductions all around, even though Alex's distress was clear. But he didn't want to be rude, and Alex wouldn't have come back from the bathroom if she wasn't okay. Would she?

Alex shook hands with the senator and her husband. "Thank you for coming."

"It was a lovely ceremony," Ramona said brightly.

"I wasn't paying attention," Alex admitted. "Also, I was up at the front, so I didn't have a great seat."

Senator Galindo chuckled nervously, clearly opting to take the comments as a joke. "I know what you mean. I remember very little about my ceremony. It went by in a blur."

That gave her husband and Phillip permission to smile through the awkwardness. Next time, maybe he should step in, smooth things over. Or not. Alex had to learn to navigate his world in her own way. He'd offered help and it was up to her to take him up on it.

Phillip bent his head toward Alex to murmur in her ear. "Feeling better?"

Her hair had been twisted into a curly fountain at her crown. With the curve of her neck exposed, the style lent her an elegance he liked. When Alex went all out, she was breathtaking. It was probably a good thing she didn't do it very often because he was having a hard time remembering all the reasons this marriage should be cold and clinical.

"Not really," she whispered back. "How soon can we leave?"

They'd talked about the importance of the reception at length and she'd agreed to the big, formal party. And he needed to treat this whole affair like a business event to keep things on an impersonal plane. But he couldn't make her stay if she wasn't feeling well. "Is it that bad? I was hoping to introduce you to some people."

"I drank ginger ale, ate some crackers and lay on the divan while Cass sponged my neck with a cold cloth. Nothing helped. But I came out anyway because I thought I'd been gone too long. I know what my job is today. It's just harder than I'd expected it to be."

The pointed comment wasn't lost on him. She was trying and it wasn't her fault the pregnancy was playing havoc with her insides. "I'm sorry. I wish I could trade places with you. The morning sickness will pass soon, right?"

The band struck up the song the wedding planner had told them would be reserved for their first dance. It was a photo-worthy, crowd-pleasing moment that Alex hadn't wanted to include. She wasn't keen on the idea of being in the spotlight as they danced solo. But he'd talked her into it, just like all the other aspects of the wedding she'd balked at.

"Not soon enough." She glanced toward the band. "Aren't we supposed to be dancing?"

Alex was being such a good sport that she deserved an out if she wanted it. "We don't have to."

"Oh, but it's our wedding." She bit her lip in that way he'd come to find adorable. "I'd like to try. If you're okay with that."

The bravery in her statement hooked Phillip in a place inside that shouldn't have been affected by simple words. How did she slide right past all his internal barriers? No other woman had ever done that. Of course, he hadn't married anyone else.

Maybe the solemnity of the occasion had got to him more than he'd realized. That was probably it. The difficulty of pushing back his emotions was messing him up. But it was only fair to Alex that he didn't spend the day dwelling on Gina. What else was he supposed to do but shut down everything inside?

"Sure. But you have to tell me if you need to stop. I'd rather not make our wedding memorable for the wrong reason."

Looked like he would get to dance with his new wife after all. It shouldn't have been a big deal. He could pretend his internal turmoil had Gina's name all over it, but this dance suddenly meant something to him.

He led Alex to the dance floor, threading through the crowd of onlookers, and honestly, he couldn't pick out one single face he recognized. They all blurred together as he took his wife into his arms and held her close, swaying slowly. She nestled into his arms, closer than appropriate for the style of music. It was supposed to be a ballroom dance that would impress and dazzle. Alex had worried she wouldn't be able to perform. He'd waved her concerns aside.

Right at this moment, he didn't care what anyone thought of either of their dancing abilities. This was their wedding. Like Alex had said. They should enjoy it regardless of the compromises that had led them here, and he planned to.

He spread his hand against the silk at her back and breathed in the scent of sugary pears. It was the same fruity flavor Alex had worn the night they'd made love, and the rub of her body against his woke up the memories in a hurry. Who was he kidding? What had led them here was a completely illogical attraction.

Pulling back a bit, he watched her as something unfolded in her expression. Her color had come back, flooding her cheeks gorgeously. Gone was the slightly glassy sheen to her eyes that had been there since the ceremony.

In its place was something wholly affecting. Wholly sensual.

Her grip on his waist tightened as awareness bled through them both. There was no mistaking the rising heat in her gaze, in her bated breath, radiating from her touch. And there was no way for her to misinterpret his body's reaction to it all, not with how closely she pressed against him.

"You look stunning," he commented hoarsely, pleased his voice had worked at all.

Her smile lanced through him. "Thanks. I wanted to. For you. It took me a long time to find a dress that wasn't too fancy but was classy enough for your crowd."

"Sweetheart, in that dress, no one here is classy enough for *you*."

She laughed softly. "Flattery will get you everywhere, Senator Edgewood."

"Really? That's the most interesting statement you've made all day, Mrs. Edgewood."

He wanted to roll that name around on his tongue some more. He didn't want it to be strange. There'd been a time when he'd been sure there would never be another Mrs. Edgewood in his life. A time when he'd cried out against the reality of having to find one.

His search had ended with the woman in his arms. He couldn't have done this with someone who had romantic expectations and stars in her eyes. Or worse, a true wife of convenience who fit his criteria to the letter and had as much personality as the paper their agreement was written on.

The real question though—whether he could do this with Alex—remained to be seen.

Her brows lifted a touch. "Oh, yeah? That was better than 'I do'?"

"They were both great," he amended as he swung Alex around with a little more gusto since she seemed to have fully recovered.

The evening was looking up. A real wedding night would make all the doubt and difficulties worth it. Solidify their partnership. Give them a chance to bond over their decisions.

The crowd applauded as the number ended and other couples streamed onto the dance floor.

"Is it time to leave yet?" he echoed and drew the laugh from her he was hoping for. "I have a sudden desire to be alone with you."

And therein lay Alex's danger. Five minutes ago, he'd been focused on the business at hand. Now he couldn't think of anything but taking her home and consummating this unconventional marriage.

She was his wife and he wanted to honor that in every sense of the word.

"That's the benefit of being the bride and groom." Her face had taken on that pregnancy glow that turned her breathtaking instead of merely beautiful. "We're expected to leave early."

Well, then. Phillip hustled Alex off the dance floor and they made a round of the room to say goodbye, but it was still a good thirty minutes before they were alone in the limousine on their way back to his house—their house now—for a brief honeymoon.

The moment they settled into the limo, Phillip turned to Alex, about to draw her into his arms. His body ached to pick up where the promises made during dancing had left off.

His wife lacked polish, connections and a comfort among his set. She hated parties and dressing up. The next few months would obviously be a difficult adjustment period for them both as they struggled to find common ground, but right this minute, he didn't care about any of that. When it was just the two of them, there was only passion. Like it had been on the night that had sealed their fate, setting them on this journey together.

At last, he'd have Alex back in his bed. The one place they made sense together. Sex worked between them. He yearned to recapture that connection.

The look at her face in the dim lighting ruined that idea.

"Sorry," she gasped. "Give me a minute. I don't—"

And then she clamped her lips together, shaking her head, looking decidedly uninterested in the type of evening activities Phillip had hoped were in store.

Based on the burn of regret in his gut, it was probably

best to stay dressed and out of bed. Intimacy had only led to complications thus far. Why would tonight be any different? He'd let his guard down, forgetting how important it was to stay detached in light of their agreement.

Phillip sighed. Maybe the Rangers were playing on TV tonight.

As weddings went, Alex's had left a lot to be desired.

Of course, she'd never sat around and daydreamed about her big day the way other women did. So the disappointment was minimal. Most of it was directed at herself. Phillip's patience was legendary, but even she could see how spectacularly she'd failed at being a politician's wife.

Thank God she hadn't actually thrown up on anyone. When he'd carried her across the threshold of his house, he'd been so sweet. But clearly didn't get the concept of how movement of any kind threatened her stomach.

Finally alone in the gargantuan bathroom attached to the bedroom she and Phillip now shared, she swiped her eyeliner and mascara off. Cass would have a heart attack if she could see Alex treating her skin so casually, but Alex wanted to lie down. Immediately.

Phillip had deposited her on the same bed where they'd given in to the heat between them after his party and wandered off to "give her some privacy."

She crawled into bed, wondering if she'd put Phillip off the idea of sleeping with her entirely. Obviously sex was out for the evening—certainly not by her choice—but surely Phillip intended to use his bed. Time ticked by. The bed swallowed her, and the masculine tone of the decorations reminded her that this had been solely a man's domain for a long time.

They'd agreed to share a bedroom and she'd thought that would start tonight. Had prepared herself for it. Had reminded herself there would be a necessary adjustment period. After all of that, where was he?

Far, far away from his wife, clearly. Because she'd ruined his opportunities for campaigning at the reception? Was he *that* mad at her?

She must have fallen asleep because something startled her awake sometime later. The dark room had a hush about it that told her she was still alone. And she was wide-awake. Her stomach was strangely settled. Of course.

No better time to feel great than the middle of the night in a new house. She hadn't officially moved in until today, though movers had brought the majority of her things yesterday. Her house was on the market, and as advised by the Realtor, she'd left the furnishings to give it more appeal to buyers. It had felt so weird to leave her house behind, almost fully intact, as if she might return to it after a long vacation. But she wouldn't be returning and it was pretty unsettling to think about new people in her house.

This was her residence now. The place where she'd raise her baby alongside Phillip. The house itself was over a hundred years old with sweeping colonial accents and artwork that should be in a museum behind glass. Certainly not a style she'd have chosen. And Phillip had three servants who lived in the converted coach house fifty yards from the flagstone side porch that flanked the west wing. Definitely not something she was used to.

She glanced at the clock. 1:00 a.m. Had Phillip fallen asleep somewhere else? Since it was her house now too, if she wanted to get up and find her husband, that was her right. If any of the servants were wandering around this late, they probably wouldn't think anything of it. Would they?

She bit her lip.

The way she felt—lost, adrift, scared—had nothing to do with what the new lady of the house should be allowed to do. She missed Phillip. Marriage was new and the house was new and being pregnant was new. She needed to not be alone right now.

Throwing on a robe as she padded to the door, Alex wandered down the hall to the ornate staircase that curved to the marble floor below. Soft, hidden lighting somewhere in the recesses of the stairs guided her path as she crept to the first floor. Otherwise, the house was dark.

Except for Phillip's study. A lamp spilled a glow into the hall through the slightly ajar door. Pushing it open, she peered over the edge of the couch, which faced away from the door and overlooked a small courtyard outside the triple bay window. Phillip indeed had fallen asleep on the couch, still dressed, still sitting up against the plush cushions.

She skirted the couch and stopped short of touching him. Her hand fell to her side as she took a moment to study this man she'd married. In sleep, his handsome face had relaxed. Normally, he had this energy about him that drew her eye…and everyone else's. Charisma was a big part of his appeal, no doubt, but in this quiet moment, she could also appreciate other subtleties, like his strength, both internal and external.

She might have leaned on that a little too hard today. But the day had been difficult. Other than her mom and bridesmaids, the crush of people at the ceremony and the reception had been Phillip's guests. And every eye had been turned on her. It had been exhausting to keep up with what little conversation she had been included in.

Then, as now, she sought the one person who was supposed to be her lifeline in this deal. Whether he was annoyed at her or not, she needed the contact. He was leaving tomorrow for Washington and they'd had precious little time together as it was, thanks to her morning sickness.

Gently, she touched his shoulder. "Come to bed."

His eyelids blinked open but he didn't immediately stand. "What are you doing here?"

She flinched and tried to catch it, but she'd never been good at hiding her thoughts. And that terse comment had not been the reception she'd anticipated. "Looking for you. I was lonely and you weren't in bed."

"For a reason," he muttered. "You should go back to sleep. You're pregnant."

Hands on her hips, she scowled down at this grumpy man she scarcely recognized. "What? *Pregnant?* When were you going to tell me about this?"

A smile tugged at his lips, though he tried to fight it. "I just meant you need your rest and I didn't want to bother you. You're sleeping for two now."

"Is that why you didn't come to bed?" The light dawned then. Maybe his absence had less to do with disappointment in her and more to do with a misguided sense of sacrifice.

"Among other reasons," he returned. "Figured it was better not to tempt fate after what happened in the limo."

The look he shot her should have been lascivious, but she sensed there was something else underneath it. Something he wasn't planning to share with her. Instead of doing as he'd practically ordered and hightailing it back upstairs, she sank onto the couch next to him. "Is it weird to think of sharing a bed?"

He shrugged without looking at her. "Not weird. Different."

How selfish was she? All this time she'd been caught up in her own fears and hang-ups, never realizing he'd stumbled into some internal roadblocks, as well.

"We don't have to," she said instantly. "There's no reason to rush things."

Perhaps it would help to give them both a bit of breathing room. She could get her bearings and figure out how to stop feeling so much like she'd stepped off the edge of a cliff with no wings. He could take some time to work through…whatever was worrying him.

Silence filled the space and she glanced at him. They'd never had trouble talking before. In fact, some of her favorite memories involved deep discussions about random subjects of which they'd always seemed to have an endless supply.

Not only was Phillip grumpy tonight, but he'd added a distance into the mix that she didn't especially like.

"Hey." Impulsively, she clasped his hand. "We're supposed to be partners. If something's bothering you, we should talk about it."

She wanted things to be like they'd been before. Was that too much to ask? Had marriage actually driven them apart? If so, that was a side effect someone should have warned her about before she'd said "I do." Regardless, she'd made a deal and she'd stick to it. She just hadn't counted on it making them both miserable.

He stared down at their joined hands for so long, she thought he wasn't going to answer. But he didn't pull away, so that was something.

"You know this is where I lived with Gina, right?" he finally asked.

His first wife. He rarely talked about her other than to say they'd been very much in love, so Alex's knowledge of the woman was limited. But she would definitely like to hear more, especially if it meant she didn't have to go back to that lonely bedroom just yet.

She nodded. "It's okay. I don't mind. We both had other lives before we met."

He flashed her a brief smile of appreciation. "That's not weird for you?"

It hadn't been until he brought it up. Should she be worried about competing with a ghost? "We talked about this last week. This is your ancestral home and I had no particular attachment to mine, so…here we are. I wouldn't say it's weird, just different."

An intentional echo of his words. Clearly they both had some adjusting to do. But for the good of the baby, they were in this together, for better or worse.

"I appreciate that. And the pass on sharing a bedroom. That is something we should probably ease into. More than anything, I want to be sure you feel like you're being treated fairly."

Fair? She wasn't being forced to raise her child alone and their marriage had the best possible basis for lasting because they'd established easy-to-follow rules up front. What wasn't fair about that? "This is still new, but I certainly don't feel like I'm being taken advantage of."

"Good. It would be hard for some women to be in a marriage of convenience with no hope of having her husband fall in love with her."

They'd had this discussion once already, but that had been before they'd actually tied the knot. Now it had a sense of finality that hadn't been there before. She was living in his house, sharing his name and pregnant with his child, but she would never have a place in his heart.

Yeah, she was okay with that. Love didn't exist. Or rather, it didn't last. Except maybe it did for some people. Phillip and his first wife obviously, and probably some other people. Cass and Gage, for example. If anyone could defy the odds and have a lasting love, her money was on those two.

She frowned. So if it lasted for some people, what if it could for her and she never had the chance to find out? That was the crux of Phillip's question. What if she woke up one day in a loveless marriage and that wasn't okay anymore?

"I signed up for no expectations, Phillip," she countered with a bravado she suddenly didn't feel. "That means I'm not expecting anything more than what we agreed to."

But that didn't mean she wasn't allowed to *hope* for something more. If Phillip had loved Gina, he obviously had the capacity for it. Maybe part of *no expectations* could be taking time to explore what could happen between Alex and her husband inside of a safe agreement. No pressure. No one scouting for the exit. No idea what it would look like. Just two people taking it slow so no one got hurt.

Maybe that was the key to getting their relationship back to the way it had been before they'd got pregnant and married. Because she wanted that easy, flirtatious camaraderie back.

If love was in the cards, that was strictly a bonus.

Six

By Sunday evening, the distance Alex sensed between her and Phillip hadn't disappeared.

He spoke. He listened. Sometimes he smiled. But he'd moved some things to a bedroom down the hall, essentially kicking himself out of his own room—which only made sense, he argued, because he was going to be in Washington most of the time. He didn't touch her, even casually, and all of their conversations skated along a very practical edge. Of course they had to talk about logistics and get used to living with each other. But did it have to be so…clinical?

It was like he'd flipped a switch.

While he packed for the trip back to Washington, Alex sat in the breakfast nook adjacent to the kitchen, a spot she'd discovered by accident, but liked very well. Franka, the stout German cook Phillip employed, had welcomed Alex into the kitchen and the two women had had a couple of friendly conversations.

Which was nice. She needed a friend in this giant house, especially now that Phillip would be gone until Friday. For the time being, he planned to commute back and forth until they could enjoy a less restrictive schedule. Alex was hoping once her morning sickness wore off, she could arrange to work remotely for three weeks a month and come home to Dallas for face-to-face meetings the fourth week. She hadn't approached Cass, Trinity and Harper about it yet, but Alex didn't anticipate much resistance to the idea. Cass did something similar since Gage lived and worked in Austin.

Cass had to drive it, though. Alex's husband owned a private jet and she intended to make full use of it. Love Field was only a few miles from their house, making plane travel a bit easier than it normally would be. Being married to a man from old oil money did have its perks.

In this day and age, nearly any business task could be managed with a cell phone, an internet connection and a laptop. Except meetings with the rest of the Senate, apparently. When Phillip had told her they'd work it out, she hadn't exactly understood that she'd be the one who had to make the most sacrifices.

It's worth it, she reminded herself. The baby would have two parents and that was what mattered.

But when Phillip hunted her down to say goodbye, he brushed her cheek with his and then headed for the airport with a cool "I'll call you." Which kind of left her wondering *why* it was worth it, especially when she spent half the night in the bathroom, hugging the floor in agony. Alone.

Alone was how she did things, she reminded herself. She *liked* solitude, or at least she used to, but something had changed.

She wanted Phillip to be *with her*. That had been the

whole point of this kind of marriage in her mind—for them to spend time together with no pressure.

When she got to work the next morning, her calendar reminded her she had a doctor's appointment on Thursday. She groaned. Somehow she'd convinced herself the appointment was today and she'd hoped to talk to the doctor about more effective remedies for morning sickness.

Because her current state was ridiculous.

Harper bounced into Alex's office, her strawberry blond curls brushing her shoulders. Normally, Fyra's chief science officer wore her hair in a no-nonsense bun to keep it away from the machines and tools in her lab.

Harper was an excellent distraction from all the angst and mood swings and general unpredictability of Alex's life. If it got her mind off Phillip, so much the better. Especially his smile as he'd danced with her at the wedding reception, which she could not erase from her brain for some reason.

"Special occasion, Dr. Livingston?" Alex asked with a nod at Harper's hairstyle.

"Dante is in town," she acknowledged with a cheeky grin. "He's taking me to lunch."

"Boring." Alex rolled her eyes, only half jesting. "When are you going on a date with someone you might actually have a chance of getting romantic with?"

Harper and Dante had been friends since freshman year in college, when they'd been paired up in chemistry. Friends with absolutely no benefits other than companionship, which put Harper in the slim minority of women who didn't notice how hot Dr. Dante Gates was underneath his horn-rimmed glasses.

"I'm not the newlywed. Not all of us are looking for love." Harper waggled her brows. "Speaking of which, do kiss and tell."

Harper plopped into a chair and perched her chin on a palm, batting her eyelashes in a very clear invitation to spill everything. Instead of a quick rejoinder about how Alex wasn't looking for love either—which Harper well knew, as she was one of the few people aware of the agreement between Alex and Phillip—tears sprang up. As they rolled down Alex's face, Harper silently rounded the desk and gathered her friend up in a fierce hug. That only made the baffling anguish inside that much worse.

"Sorry," Alex choked out. "It's just hormones."

Probably. Harper didn't let go, but Alex didn't mind. Disappointment over Phillip's distance had caught up to her, increasing the flood exponentially. Which was ridiculous. Alex had entered Phillip's agreement willingly because it made sense. There was no room for emotional outbursts just because she'd hoped they'd pick up where they'd left off after the party. Last weekend should have been a honeymoon of sorts, even though they'd opted to skip any kind of trip because it seemed too traditional and sentimental.

The weekend had been nothing of the kind. Granted, she'd been nauseous pretty much the whole time.

But they could have spent time together. As friends. Oh, she understood that Phillip had to go to Washington for work during the week. But while he'd been home yesterday, she'd have been happy to watch a movie together or go to dinner. She didn't have to eat, but the conversation would have been nice. That would have tided her over until he came home.

But that hadn't even been suggested. Did he not think about their one night of passion the way she did? Because she wanted a repeat of their closeness, the tender kisses and their bodies communicating so perfectly.

More tears rushed down her face.

If you couldn't cry all over your best friends, who could you cry on? She and Harper had been friends since college. Way before they were business partners and colleagues.

When the surge had passed, Harper eased back and leaned on the desk, but she kept Alex's hand in hers. "That didn't seem like pregnancy hormones to me. Not that I'd know or anything."

What should have been a throwaway comment made by a staunch workaholic came out sounding wistful. As if Harper wished she could commiserate instead of merely being sympathetic.

Alex glanced at her friend through watery, suspicious eyes. "Trust me, you would not like to have firsthand knowledge, if that's what you're thinking."

"Oh, I'm not," Harper insisted with a forced laugh that raised Alex's concern even more. "I'm a scientist. I like to deal in facts. Since I've never been pregnant, I can't speak from personal experience, nor have I done any research. I mean, I know the basics and pregnancy can cause mood swi—"

"It's hormones," Alex interrupted before she got a full discourse on the potential side effects of pregnancy. "You were at the reception. Things did not improve and it's just not how I envisioned spending the weekend after my wedding. Phillip left to go back to DC yesterday."

"Oh. So no kiss and tell." Harper managed to look sympathetic through her disappointment, largely owing to her Irish charm, no doubt. "That would make me cry, too."

"It's hormones," Alex repeated through gritted teeth and one last tear trickled down to belie the statement. Crying on your friends wasn't cool if you were going to turn around and fib through your teeth about the genesis of the waterworks. "And okay, I'm sad that he's gone. Don't make a big deal out of it."

Saying it out loud made it real. Her marriage was forty-eight hours old and as lifeless as the paper it was written on. Maybe that was the deal she'd signed up for but, hormones or not, in the cold light of Monday morning it sounded as appealing as drinking dishwater.

Alex had a gorgeous husband, one who had been featured in magazine after magazine as one of the hottest bachelors in America. Now he was hers. Yet not hers. Was it so bad to dream of him taking her to bed and then calling the next day to say how much he hated that they were in different states?

"There's nothing wrong with missing your husband. I'm pretty sure that's allowed, even if you do have weird ideas about why to get married. Not that I'd know anything about that, either." Harper made a face, and if Alex didn't know better, she'd swear that jealousy laced the other woman's tone.

"Please. Phillip and I got married because of the baby." And a multitude of other reasons. "What better reason could there be? I'll be fine. I didn't have a husband last week either, so nothing has changed."

Everything had changed. That was the problem. And she had no idea what to do about it.

"Anything I can do?" Harper asked.

"You can distract me from my misery by telling me you found a new supplier for the pumice microbeads in your exfoliating scrub," Alex reminded Harper with raised eyebrows. The sooner they got off the subject of Phillip, the better. "Our profit margin is circling the drain."

"Are you that miserable? You should call your obstetrician." With a pat on Alex's arm, Harper leaned forward, clearly hoping to avoid the topic of suppliers and cost of goods.

"I have an appointment Thursday. I can suffer in silence until then. Now, about the pumice supp—"

"I'll go with you," Harper interjected smoothly. "To the appointment. Let me drive you."

"I can drive myself—" Alex sighed as she cut herself off. Maybe she spent so much time alone because she constantly drove people away. After all, it wasn't like she'd said anything to Phillip about spending time together. He probably didn't even know she'd hoped to. "You know what? That sounds nice."

"It's a date, then," Harper said. "Cass called a meeting this afternoon to talk about her progress on finding the leak, or lack thereof. Check your calendar. She just scheduled it."

Alex groaned. Someone in Fyra had leaked information to the media about Formula-47, which had nearly cost the company everything. Since they hadn't found the culprit yet, they'd decided to go forward with obtaining FDA approval before Harper felt ready, strictly to stave off damaging effects of the leak.

Another meeting with little progress. It was maddening. "Okay, thanks for the heads-up."

Back to business. That was a good way to get her mind off Phillip. Except she had a suspicion it wouldn't work.

Alex didn't exactly suffer in silence until Thursday. It was a little difficult when Fyra's chief science officer had taken on a personal mission to check on Alex ten times a day. Harper's pointed, yet loving, questions were hard to ignore, especially when Alex craved companionship. Alex found herself being honest about how she felt—physically at least, as the angst about Phillip was too hard for her to justify to herself, let alone to someone else. And she even let Harper run to 7-Eleven to fetch ginger ale a couple of times. On Thursday, true to her word, Harper popped into Alex's office, keys in hand, to drive her to the doctor.

"Let's go," Harper chirped and steered Alex into the two-seater Mercedes her friend had recently bought.

The smell of new car and leather engulfed Alex as she settled into the seat. "Thanks. For being there. I didn't realize how much I'd need hand-holding."

"Sure. That's what friends are for." Harper had tamed her red curls into a bun today, returning her to a more serious look.

Of her three business partners, Alex had always had the most in common with Harper, as they both approached life analytically. They'd had matching T-shirts in college that read Left-Brained Women Are Sexier. No one but the two of them had thought the saying was funny.

Thank God Alex had her friends during this challenging period. It didn't fully alleviate the loneliness of a big empty house, but Alex had solved that problem by going into the office early and staying until 10:00 p.m. Numbers were her refuge; always had been.

Phillip had called, as promised, every night at 10:30 p.m. and asked how she was feeling. It was nice that he took the time, but she was usually exhausted, so their conversations had been short. She then fell into Phillip-laced dreams, where he held her during the night and stroked her hair, then her skin. His lips would seek out the hollow of her throat and their urgency would increase until they were both naked and panting each other's names.

Hormones. They were killing her.

When the time for her appointment came, Alex's obstetrician, Dr. Dean, listened to her concerns about the severity of her morning sickness. "I'd like to do an ultrasound."

Dr. Dean had mentioned on Alex's first visit that she

didn't typically do ultrasounds until around eighteen weeks to verify the baby was growing correctly, and also to determine gender, which Alex very much wanted to know ahead of time.

"An ultrasound? But I'm only at eleven weeks," Alex said as her pulse started hammering in her throat. "Is something wrong? Is that why you want to do one?"

Dr. Dean waved at the nurse to roll the ultrasound machine over to the examination table and smiled at Alex. "I guess that depends on your definition of *wrong*. One explanation for the severity of your symptoms might be twins. An ultrasound will tell us, and if you are carrying multiples, finding out sooner is best."

"Twins?" All the blood rushed from Alex's head as Harper clapped gleefully from her spot across the room. "Oh, my God."

One baby felt like a huge enough responsibility to raise without damaging him or her. But two babies?

The sonographer pulled up Alex's gown, poured warm goop on her abdomen and then rolled the wide white wand across Alex's stomach. The black-and-gray screen near the table blurred and shifted with each movement and a blobby thing appeared.

Alex's heart stopped, and when it started beating again, it was too big and tight for her chest.

"Is that the baby?" Alex whispered, eyes wide so she didn't miss anything.

Phillip should be here. He should be holding her hand and watching this miracle unfold with her. Her throat ached with emotions she couldn't name, and she wished he'd care enough to be here to experience all of this, too.

"Yes," the sonographer confirmed, grinning. "And there's the other one. Dizygotic twins, or in layman's terms, fraternal. See how there are two distinct placentas?"

Twins. Alex's eyelids fluttered closed and then she pried them open to watch the sonographer type into the machine. Xs and dotted lines appeared.

"We're measuring their size so we can monitor growth," she explained. "Dr. Dean will want to do more ultrasounds as you progress to ensure we don't have an imbalance."

Alex nodded, too overwhelmed to speak. *Babies.* She had two babies in there sloshing around and causing so much havoc with her stomach. No wonder.

"So that explains your severe morning sickness," Dr. Dean said gently. "That's good news. Means nothing more serious is wrong. You'll probably start to feel better by about twelve or thirteen weeks, so not long now."

The doctor wrapped up the appointment with some additional tips and instructions and answered all of Alex's and Harper's questions. When Alex sank back into the seat of Harper's Mercedes, she let her head fall back against the headrest, too weary to think. Harper chatted about how great the news was all the way back to Fyra, and Alex let her talk, mostly because she couldn't get a word in edgewise. And her throat was too tight to make a sound.

Back in her office, she debated how to break the news to Phillip. There was no telling how he'd react. It was a reality they'd never even contemplated. Would they have to hire two nannies now? Have two nurseries—or did parents of twins typically put them in the same room?

In the end, it didn't matter. Phillip didn't answer his phone, even though she called him four times, fifteen minutes apart. Finally, she sent him a text message:

Went to the dr today. Guess what? It's twins.

Phillip was going to get his full-blown family much sooner than he'd anticipated.

* * *

When Phillip finally walked out of a three-hour meeting, the only thing he wanted to do was get something hot to eat and cold to drink. He grabbed his phone and briefcase from his office and waved to his admin, Linda, as he left Capitol Hill for the day.

The week had crawled by. Barely an hour had gone by that he hadn't thought about Alex, what she was doing, whether she felt better, if she was getting used to living at his house. He'd picked up his phone four or five times to send her a funny text message, like he'd done when they were still dancing around the edges of their attraction.

And then he'd remembered. They weren't flirting with the intent to eventually take it up a notch; they were married. In name only. She'd agreed to it and seemed pretty happy with the status quo as best he could tell during their nightly conversations, which he'd forced himself to cut short. Their relationship needed distance if it was going to work.

Of course, the distance wasn't working so well for him. Every night, he would end the call and stare at the ceiling until he fell asleep, fighting the urge to call her back so he could hear her voice again. She needed to sleep, not hang out with him on the phone for no other reason than he suddenly hated the quietness of the DC condo that had always been perfectly fine before.

One more day of Washington and then he'd fly home. Somehow, he'd have to figure out how to maintain that distance while they were in the same house. It was a horrible catch-22 to want to spend time with his new wife and yet have an inner voice reminding him that the only reason he had a new wife was because Gina had died. He'd married Alex but it didn't mean he'd moved on. Not at all. Guilt weighed down his soul to the point where some mornings, he'd had a hard time getting out of bed.

Randy opened the back door of his town car and Phillip slid into the seat with a glance at his phone. Speaking of his new wife…looked like he'd missed a bunch of calls from Alex. Frowning, he noted a text message, too. Hopefully nothing was wrong.

And then the word *twins* leaped off the screen.

"Randy, change of plans," he croaked as he tapped furiously through the message app to see if she'd sent any follow-up texts. Nothing. "Drive me to the airport. I'm flying home to Dallas unexpectedly."

Twins.

The flight home took a million years, during which Phillip questioned every single decision he'd made since the first moment he walked into Fyra and saw the barefaced woman in jeans named Alex. They were having *twins.*

And Alex had found out at a doctor's visit he hadn't been asked to attend.

That was not okay.

These were his *children*. Alex was his wife. He wanted to be involved in everything, no matter how small, and he'd been robbed of that chance for some reason. He wanted to know why. Why hadn't she told him she was going to the doctor? Why hadn't she wanted him there?

The pilot announced the aircraft had entered Dallas airspace. Finally.

Phillip whipped off his seat belt the moment the wheels hit the tarmac and glared at Randy as his driver, who always traveled with him, lumbered to his feet a good thirty seconds after the plane had rolled to a stop. All Phillip had to do was raise his eyebrows for the man to clue in that time was of the essence.

"Where to, boss?" Randy asked mildly as they double-timed it to the private lot where Phillip kept his car. Normally, Randy pulled the car onto the tarmac and loaded Phillip's luggage when they returned home, but his driver had figured out that normal wasn't the theme of this trip. Plus, Phillip didn't have any luggage since he hadn't taken time to go back to his condo.

Phillip glanced at his watch. Nearly 9:00 p.m. Dallas time, a near miracle considering he'd climbed into his car at Capitol Hill just before six DC time. "To the house."

Where Alex would be at home, hopefully eating whatever Franka had made. Whatever Alex wanted, spare no expense or effort, he'd told Franka. Of course, he hadn't known his wife was eating for three then or he might have thrown Franka a side comment about watching Alex's nutrition, as well. He should have anyway.

Randy drove like a demon possessed, which Phillip appreciated, but when they got to the house, George met Phillip at the door with a puzzled frown. "Sir? We didn't expect you unt—"

"Where's Alex?" Phillip blew through the door, his gaze already searching the floor above. "She's not already in bed, is she?"

"Not hardly." George clucked, displeasure lacing his tone. "Ms. Alexandra is still at her office."

A spurt of anger ripped through Phillip's breastbone. "She's…what?"

"At work," George repeated, but Phillip had already spun to march back down the steps.

Not only pregnant, but with twins…and still at work? She should be working reduced hours, not putting her nose to the grindstone. If he had his way, she'd be sitting on the couch at home reading a book instead of working even eight hours a day, let alone fourteen. And she'd let Phillip take care of her. He wanted to.

By the time Randy pulled up at the glass-and-brick building housing Fyra Cosmetics, Phillip's temper had well passed the unreasonable stage. He and his wife had some words to exchange.

Fishing his guest security badge from his briefcase, Phillip launched from the car and stormed through the reception area, pausing long enough—just barely—to beep through the glass door leading to the executive offices.

Light spilled from the door marked Chief Financial Officer. The moment he stepped across the threshold, he opened his mouth to blast Alex.

Clearly startled, she glanced up, and as her gaze lit on him, it filled with something so warm and so tender, all his breath rushed from his lungs. Her wide smile poleaxed him in the stomach, and all of that was so definitely *not* what he'd expected that he forgot everything he'd planned to say.

His wife was so beautiful. And she was the mother of his babies. It was nearly divine how she'd suddenly filled him to the brim.

"Phillip!" She shot to her feet and rounded the desk with her arms spread as if she meant to fly into his embrace, and then, all at once, she skidded to a stop just short, her gaze hungrily taking him in. "I wasn't expecting you."

"Clearly not," he said gruffly, taken aback at how disappointed he was that she'd stopped.

What the hell.

He pulled her into his arms for what should have been a quick hug between parents…friends…spouses…whatever they were. But then she nestled in with a sigh, setting his blood on a simmer that completely changed the mood. His arms tightened and he held her, breathing in the scent of her hair.

"I guess you got my message," she murmured. "I tried to call."

"I know. I was in a meeting." It sounded as inane to his ears as it probably did to hers. He pulled back to zero in on her face. "Why didn't you tell me you had a doctor's appointment?"

"Oh." Confusion marred her beautiful bare face. "I didn't think you'd care. It was just a doctor's appointment. I have a lot of those. Goes with the territory."

"Of course I care." His voice was still gruff from the long day. Or something. "Especially if you're going to have an ultrasound. You have to tell me about these things."

"I didn't know. It was just a routine checkup, but when I mentioned how bad my morning sickness still was, Dr. Dean wanted to see if I was carrying twins." She shot him a wry smile. "I guess that's why they pay her the big bucks, because she called it in one."

"So it's true?" he whispered and his hand moved to Alex's abdomen involuntarily, as if he could validate by touching her that not one but two heartbeats lay just on the other side of her skin.

She pressed into his hand and the moment intensified as they stared at each other. He wasn't just touching the babies, but *her*. And she felt amazing under his palm. Everything in the world could vanish except for what was in his grasp and he'd be all right with that.

"It's true. I saw the pictures myself," she murmured, her gaze going soft and bright. "Oh, I have them."

She ducked out of his embrace and crossed to her desk, pulled open a drawer and rummaged around until she triumphantly held up a few pieces of paper.

She handed them to him and he glanced down at the black-and-white squares. Ultrasound pictures. And *there they were*. Two light-colored blobs in circles, surrounded by darkness. His babies. *Their* babies.

His eyes stung. *Stung*, like he might actually shed a tear. Why hadn't someone prepared him for this moment when he got to see his children for the first time? It wouldn't have mattered; he wouldn't have listened because how could he have prepared for *this*? The swell of his heart, the spike of his pulse. The sheer awe. All of it poured through him thickly and he couldn't have spoken to save his life.

"It's pretty amazing, huh?" she asked softly and he took it as a rhetorical question because of course the answer was yes. "I wish you'd been there to see them move."

"Me too." Apparently he *could* talk. "I'm going to be there next time. I want advance notice of all doctor's appointments from now on."

"Okay. I'm glad you want to be involved. I thought…" She trailed off and bit her lip. "Well, when you left on Sunday, I got the impression we weren't supposed to share things. I would have said something, but you seemed… distracted every time we talked. It almost felt like you were avoiding me."

Of course she'd thought that. His quest for distance had been a stellar success. So much so that he'd missed an important step in Alex's pregnancy because of his own boneheadedness. Paper rustled under his fingers as his hands tightened into fists. Carefully, he set down the ultrasound pictures before he crumpled them.

"I'm sorry you thought that. I wasn't trying to avoid you." Yeah, he kind of had been, but now it didn't make any sense. Either they were partners and friends or there was no reason to be married. He wanted her to feel like she could tell him things. He wanted to know about her and not just about the pregnancy.

The Distance Plan wasn't going to work. He needed a new plan in order to make this marriage succeed. Otherwise, they'd both be miserable.

"Won't it be hard to come to doctor's appointments when you're in Washington?" she asked and it was a perfectly logical question.

Yes, it would be difficult but he didn't care. He couldn't stand the thought of missing one more second of his wife's pregnancy. Of missing his wife.

Where had *that* come from? That wasn't the point here.

"Let me worry about that. Now, let's talk about what time it is and why you're still at work, shall we?" The subject change flowed out smoothly, a plus considering he'd started out this little interlude as a confrontation. And somehow, she'd got him all discombobulated with a simple smile.

She had the grace to look chagrined. "I wasn't expecting you to catch me."

"Ah, so you recognize that it's a problem for a woman in your condition to work herself too hard."

Good. Maybe this would end up being a reasonable conversation about what a woman expecting twins could and couldn't do. Back on track, he smiled gently.

"What? No." She shook her head with a scowl. "What kind of 'condition' would that be, Phillip? I'm pregnant, not incompetent. I know my limits."

Except clearly she didn't. "Then why the guilty face?"

"Because I—" She looked away, biting her lip again. A dead giveaway that she had something on her mind that she didn't want to say. "I didn't want to go home."

"You hate my house? You can't sleep? What is it? You can say it."

She was hesitating because she knew she was guilty as charged. She should be at home with her feet up, letting him cater to her every whim. She deserved to be treated like a queen and to have a husband around who could look after her well-being. Which would be hard for him to do in Washington, as well.

How had everything got so complicated?

"It's too empty," she blurted out. "I don't like being there alone."

He waved it off. "You're not alone. I have a full staff—"

"*You're* not there, Phillip! I don't like being at the house without you. I work until ten so I can go home and fall into bed, so exhausted that I don't think about how you left Sunday with barely a goodbye. I missed you. I miss the way we were before *this*—" she sliced at her midsection "—happened. Why can't the pregnancy be something that brings us together?"

A lone tear rolled down her face and the sight of it clenched his gut. The emotional distance he'd created wasn't working so well. For either of them. She'd been working late because he hadn't been engaging her as a person, as the future mother of his children.

This was his fault and he needed to fix it, before the damage to his marriage became irreparable.

Here, in the light of these revelations, it didn't seem so terrible to admit that he wanted to be with her. To hold her whenever he felt like it and let her do the same. The distance he'd created hadn't done what he'd hoped anyway. He still thought about Alex, still wanted her in his bed.

The Distance Plan sucked. New plan—make Alex glad she'd married him. Get back to where they'd been before the babies came into the picture. Be real friends and partners. Back to Basics. That was a great new plan. Hopefully along the way, he'd earn the right to be included in things like ultrasounds. The only thing he didn't have quite worked out yet was how he'd get closer to Alex and keep his commitment to Gina's memory.

But he had to. Somehow.

Seven

The first thing Phillip did when they got home was draw Alex a bath.

The second thing he did was insist she get in it while he made her a tray of tea and crackers.

After the emotional breakdown in her office, Alex had half expected Phillip to jet back to Washington. They didn't have a real marriage; theirs was based on rules. She got that, knew what she'd signed up for. The whole time she'd been admitting how much she missed him, she knew she shouldn't be, that it was a risky move, but there was no way she could have held back, not with Phillip within arm's length. Not when she was still so raw from his sudden appearance and the way he'd held her and touched her.

And yet Phillip hadn't fled. He was here, in the house, with no apparent plans to leave. Maybe that meant an opportunity to change things. But how? And to what? Alex wasn't one to jump in with both feet. Except for that one time at the party, and look where that had got her.

Bubbles up to her neck, Alex relaxed in the giant oval bathtub as best she could under the circumstances. The bathtub might be her favorite spot in the house. It was on a raised platform with windows surrounding it, and the bathtub overlooked a cheerful garden. At night, the garden's floodlights cast the bathroom in a dim, rosy glow. The day's stresses melted away.

And then Phillip bustled in, tray in hand. Gorgeous, self-assured, and oh so very sexy with his shirtsleeves rolled to midforearm and dark hair rumpled from his flight.

"I, uh…didn't know you were coming in," she squeaked.

She was naked under these bubbles. And her husband didn't seem too worried about it as he crossed over to the pale marble tub and perched on the wide lip. Carefully, he placed the tray of tea and saltines next to him on the ledge and slid it out of the way, toward the wall.

"Well, I wasn't planning on it, but that water does look tempting." His lips quirked as he let his gaze travel down the length of the tub, which consisted of nothing but bubbles. The sudden heat flashing through his expression made her wonder if he could see more than she assumed.

But then…he'd seen her naked before, so what was she freaking out about? And she'd been dreaming of the day he wanted to see her naked again. If today was that day, she didn't want to breathe too hard in case she blew away her chance to be with Phillip again.

"I meant, I didn't know you were coming into the bathroom," she corrected hastily. Did she sound as breathless to him as she did to herself? "Men don't like baths."

"As a rule, I suppose, but other men don't have you in their bathtubs." Lazily, he swirled a finger through the bubbles as he watched her. "Lucky for me I'm not other men."

It sure looked like he might be seriously contemplating

joining her. Was he going to dive right into the tub? Oh, my, she certainly hoped so.

She didn't know where to put her hands. "There's enough room for two."

Her cheeks burned as she envisioned Phillip stripping down and sliding against the marble, his skin slick against hers. Then he'd touch her and they'd fall back into the way they'd been at the party. Connected. Hot. Meaningful.

That was all she wanted—his attention on her like it had been then, so focused and delicious. No rules, just two people who wanted to be together.

His grin lit her up inside. "That's the best invitation I've had all week. But not now. This evening is about you and you only. I want to take care of you. If I got into that tub, all my good intentions would go out the window."

Now she couldn't decide if she was disappointed or intrigued. Maybe a little of both. "That sounds interesting. Tell me more about that."

Something wicked flashed through his expression. "You want to hear about how easily you could break down my good intentions? I didn't know you liked dirty talk, Mrs. Edgewood."

"I haven't heard any yet, so I honestly don't know if I'd like it," she countered primly, trying hard to be shocked at her own boldness and failing miserably.

She'd married this man to provide a family and future for her children. That didn't mean she had to live alone, be lonely or pretend she didn't want him. In fact, she didn't recall any rules against that.

"Well, see… I wanted to rub your feet." He punctuated this comment by dipping a hand in the water and fishing her ankle from the suds. Then he held it in his palm as he kneaded her instep with a thumb. "Like this. Thought you might enjoy it."

She was too busy groaning at the exquisite sensations radiating through her foot. Why hadn't she realized her feet hurt that bad? "You can do that. I don't mind."

"Oh, I had all these *good intentions* to massage your whole body." He picked up her other foot and began to rub it in kind. Her eyelids fluttered closed involuntarily. "I was about to launch into a very long description of how I'd taste your whole body if I got into that tub with you."

Every inch of her went liquid as that promise exploded in her core. Caught between the tantalizing glimpse of what could be and the amazing things currently happening to her body, her brain wasn't too quick on the draw.

"You twisted it all around," she murmured as her head sank back against the marble. "I wanted to hear about how you planned to take care of me."

"One and the same, Alex." His low voice drifted through her. "Or at least it is now. Because every second I'm seeing to your comfort, my hands will be on you. And I'll be thinking about how taking care of you might include something pleasurable for us both."

That she could get on board with in a hurry. Something had changed. She could sense it, as if he'd opened up. And now that she had his attention, she could admit, to herself at least, how much she'd craved it, how her body cried for his touch.

"I definitely want to hear more about that."

"How about I show you instead?"

Wordlessly, he found her hand and gently pulled her out of the bubbles until she was standing in the water, bared to him. Droplets of water and suds slid along the planes of her body, sensitizing it. His gaze followed the drops, lingering along the way, and that heightened the heat blooming along her skin.

Phillip grabbed a towel and dried her carefully, murmuring about how beautiful she was. He dropped flowery phrases as he worked, turning the utilitarian act of drying skin into a seduction. Her starving soul ate up the words, hiding them away. Her neglected body soaked up his touch. Everything felt bigger, better, stronger than the last time she'd been naked with Phillip.

Her left brain recognized that pregnancy hormones were heightening the experience. Her everything else couldn't wait to find out what the rest of it was going to feel like.

"Phillip," she said hoarsely. "Take me to bed."

His hand stilled on her back. "Are you sure? No morning sickness tonight?"

The questions lingered in the air. He was giving her a chance to back out if this wasn't what she wanted. A chance to analyze where this step in their relationship might lead, and he was okay if she used morning sickness as an excuse. She appreciated that more than he could possibly know. It meant he understood she didn't normally throw caution to the wind—and he wanted her to make the choice.

"None. Finish what we never got to start the night of our wedding." Actually, she hadn't even thought about her stomach since the moment he'd walked into Fyra earlier that evening.

He grinned and picked her up easily, snugging her into his arms as he nuzzled her ear. "You sure you don't want that massage?"

She nestled into his embrace. Strong. Capable. It was a good thing she wasn't standing because her knees had just gone weak. "I thought I was promised both."

"And both you shall have."

He carried her to the bed and laid her out on it, worshipping her with his gaze.

She shivered under the onslaught, though he hadn't

touched her again. His eyes on her were enough as he swept her from head to toe with that heated contemplation.

She'd forgotten how nice that felt. Phillip made her feel beautiful, even when she had nothing on her face. Her company had been built on the premise that a woman required enhancements to be attractive, to gain the attention of a lover. She'd never thought it worked, that it *should* work. If a man wanted you, he should want the woman you were, not the woman you pretended to be.

It was her shameful secret. She owed Cass so much, owed Trinity and Harper for taking her in despite her juvenile arrest record. How could Alex tell her friends that cosmetics made no sense to her?

Here under the laser-sharp, watchful eye of Phillip, she didn't have to pretend. He knew she didn't like dressing up and he didn't care. The way his gaze perused her naked body said he liked what he saw. That was so powerful.

"I hope you're planning to join me in the bed," she murmured. "The bath was one thing, but I'm pretty sure the activities I had in mind require you to get wet this time."

His brows shot up but he schooled the shock off his face. "Why, Mrs. Edgewood. Is that a sample of the dirty talk you mentioned earlier? I wasn't aware you planned to be the one doing the talking but I'm in favor of it."

"More where that came from," she promised as the sound of his voice calling her Mrs. Edgewood curled up in her belly, warming her. Strange. Who would have thought a simple title could be so affecting? Must be the way he'd said it, with a slightly naughty edge.

Whatever had shifted between them got her vote. She just wished she knew what it was. So if things shifted the other way again, she could fix it.

With a small chuckle, Phillip began shedding his clothes. She watched, shamelessly. Of course, she'd seen him naked too, but that had been months ago…and pre-whacked-out hormones, obviously, because she really didn't remember the sight of his fingers slipping buttons free of their moorings being so erotic.

But as the second one popped out, something sharp stabbed through her core, heating her from the inside out. Third one, fourth, and the heat flushed upward to encompass her torso, spreading to her breasts, peaking them.

He watched her just as shamelessly as she watched him, his eyes growing darker the more her body visibly reacted.

"You're a fan of stripteases, too?" he asked, his voice rough with appreciation. "That's incredibly hot."

His shirt was as unbuttoned as it could be, baring his chest. And then he slid it off, first one shoulder, then the other. It shouldn't have been so—*wow*.

"It's news to me, as well," she muttered as her back arched involuntarily. "Don't you dare stop."

"I wouldn't dream of it. I find myself anxious to explore all the interesting things going on with your body." His hands had moved to his pants and the zipper released with a quick tug. Then, as he shoved the fabric away, catching his briefs in the same motion, she got a good eyeful of how she'd been affecting him thus far.

Oh, my. She wanted that gorgeous length of flesh. Right now. That pleasure he'd promised her had already started in a very big way and she ached to finish it.

Silently, she held out her hands and he fell onto the bed next to her, drawing her into his arms a bit roughly, but she didn't mind. His body felt heavenly against hers, insistent, hard, hot. All of it inflamed her to the point of senselessness and a moan fell from her lips as he thrust a thigh between her legs.

He took her mouth with his in an urgent kiss that grew exponentially more heated every second. Their tongues clashed, seeking, tasting, feeling, and she nearly bucked off the bed when his hands found her breasts. He molded them to his palms, explored them as he'd told her he would, and the ache at her core morphed into something almost agonizing. She needed him more than she'd ever needed anything.

"Hurry," she mouthed against his lips and rocked her hips against his for emphasis.

"I don't think I could do it another way," he muttered as her fingers closed around his gloriously hard shaft. "And this will be over if you keep that up."

With a groan, he removed her hand and rolled her to her back. Then he kissed his way down the length of her body, spread her thighs and put his mouth in the center of the heat she couldn't contain.

The first wet touch of his tongue nearly split her apart. She might have screamed as sensation rocketed through her body. Her hips bucked against his mouth as he pleasured her and that tight coil of need spun faster and faster until it exploded in a storm of light behind her eyes.

Her whole body stiffened as she cried out his name, and then he was kissing her gently, holding her tight against him as she rode out the thick waves of release. No words. No bones. Her whole body might have disintegrated in the aftermath and she didn't care.

He let her recover—not fully, because that was frankly impossible, but enough. His hands threaded through her hair as he cupped the back of her head, drawing her face close to his so he could nibble on her lips, then her throat, and the whole tide started over again.

But this time, he murmured more flowery phrases as he kissed her, and when he poised between her thighs, ready to claim her a second time, he captured her gaze, watching her intently as he pushed inside.

The connection electrified her, sensitized her, heightened her pleasure as his blue eyes went hot. They were joined and it was magnificent, much more so than the first time. With no condom between them, it took less than a minute for her to crest that peak again.

He shuddered with his own release and they both went limp in each other's arms, torsos heaving and neither in a hurry to drift apart. His palms smoothed across her buttocks, cradling her close, and something so raw and elemental broke open inside her, she could barely breathe.

The same thing had happened when she'd shown him the ultrasound pictures... His awed, perfect reaction had touched something deep inside. The look on his face had floored her, rushing through her, awakening parts of her she didn't know existed. Kind of like now.

She'd ignored it then. But couldn't have in this moment for a million dollars. Her emotions were fully engaged in this relationship, despite her best effort to stick with what was logical, and she wanted things, so many things. Things she didn't know how to express. Things that scared her because she'd been convinced none of them were real.

Right now, all of them were oh so real.

She couldn't let go of Phillip. Didn't want to let go. But she should.

None of this internal catch-22 should have been happening just because they'd had sex. Sex had been part of the agreement. They were married; of course they were going to take care of each other's needs.

The reality? Not the nice, safe marital bed she'd imagined. Actually, nothing about her marriage had gone like she'd thought it would. The confusion and swirl of uncertainty nearly overwhelmed her, and all she wanted to do to soothe it was cling to Phillip. The author of her alarm. What was she supposed to do with that?

For his part, he seemed sated and content to lie there murmuring lovely things about round two in her ear as he stroked her hair. Maybe he was onto something. There was no cause for panic. She could stay focused on how good they made each other feel and forget about stuff she couldn't explain.

Her marriage would work because they'd both agreed to keep emotions out of it. The rules were there for a reason. Rules kept you from getting hurt and from hurting other people. Rules kept the subject of divorce at bay.

Besides, Phillip didn't believe in second chances. He'd married the great love of his life already, and there was no room for Alex in his heart. If only… No. That was the opening phrase of a path straight to madness.

But as she lay in Phillip's arms, cradled by the husband she'd never planned to have, pregnant with the babies she'd never imagined being gifted with, her heart started filling in the blank without her permission.

The Back to Basics Plan might be the best one Phillip had ever devised.

When sunlight filtered through the drawn curtains, he'd already been awake for a while, just listening to Alex breathe. Even that was a turn-on.

If only he could wake her up with a kiss and dive in again. But he resisted. Barely. She needed her sleep, especially since she'd been working until ten o'clock. The woman needed a good spanking. Among other things. His imagination got busy thinking up additional wicked items for that list.

And now he had an erection the size of the Senate chambers. Where he should currently be but wasn't because he'd flown home on a whim to have it out with his wife about her bad habits. Guess he'd skipped over that confrontation in favor of something much more necessary.

His marriage was on much better ground than it had been. Fortunately. Some things were worth the sacrifice, and Alex, the mother of his twins, definitely was. He sent Linda a text message, begging her to cover for him at Capitol Hill, and tossed his phone back on the nightstand. On Silent.

The government could do without a senator for one day.

Alex sighed and rolled over, facing him. Her eyes were still closed, her body relaxed in sleep. Even in the dim light of the rising sun, he could see the line of her hip and the length of her legs as they stretched toward the footboard.

Gina had always slept curled in a ball, one hand over her face, as if to ward off the darkness. Since she'd died, he sometimes woke up in the middle of the night and, in that half second of semiconsciousness, could feel Gina's presence in the bed. It was always so real he'd have a moment of panic when he couldn't find her.

And then reality would wash over him with biting, bitter coldness. She was gone. Irrevocably. In those moments, it felt like his heart had been clawed from his chest and buried with her.

A part of him wondered why he didn't bring home a new woman every night in an attempt to ward off such a visceral nighttime experience. But he couldn't. He hadn't let other women into his bed except very briefly, and then he always escorted them home after. Alex was the first to still be there in the morning.

He'd put off sleeping with her overnight, hoping to assuage the guilt before it affected the friendship they were developing, but he'd known marrying Alex meant she'd eventually fill the empty space.

And now that it had happened…it was so much better

than he'd imagined. Better than he'd planned to allow. His chest hurt with the conflict waging an all-out war inside. He wanted to embrace what he had with Alex, and what it might become, but how could he? It was so disloyal to Gina he could hardly breathe.

Alex blinked awake and smiled. "You owe me. I never got tea or a massage last night."

That pulled a laugh from him in spite of all the turmoil seething under his skin. "And here I thought what I did give you made up for losing out on those."

Nodding, her smile widened. "Mmm, yes. Good point. I'll give you a pass on both."

All at once, she stretched one arm over her head and the sheet slipped down. One rosy nipple popped free of the covers, drawing his eye. Her breasts had grown fuller, lusher since the party and he obviously hadn't paid enough attention to them last night because his mouth started watering as he pondered tasting them again.

He snaked an arm out and gathered her against him in one motion. Sex made sense. It was a release and then over. No disloyal emotional commitment involved.

"Oh, no," he said smoothly over her squeal. "You're far too quick to forgive. I promised you a massage. And tea. But we'll get to the tea later."

Her gaze filled with heat instantly, her eyelids dropping a touch as she tangled her legs with his, aligning their hips to bring her dampness flush with his hard-on. Yes, that would do nicely. Last night, he'd been so focused on her pleasure that he'd ignored his own needs.

This morning, he'd sate himself. As soon as he made sure the coast was clear.

He bent his head and nuzzled her ear. "You're feeling okay this morning?"

"Very okay," she purred and fused her lips to his, drawing him into a kiss that spiraled out of control in a heartbeat.

He groaned as her skin ignited his. He didn't remember her being this way before they'd got married. Hot, sure. Willing, absolutely. But this was different, an urgency he could barely keep up with. Though he'd give it the college try.

Tearing his mouth from hers, he treated himself to those gorgeous breasts, massaging them with his tongue as promised. But she arched against his mouth, moaning with little sighs that drove him crazy, and then got her hips in on the action, writhing against him.

One small shift of his hips and they joined.

It was insanely perfect. Beautiful. They fit together better than anything he could have imagined and he reveled in it for a moment, too overcome to break the spell. Alex was in his arms, hair spread over his pillow, and she was so much more than the wife he'd thought he needed, he could hardly reconcile it all.

With a sound, she rolled her hips, taking her own pleasure, apparently too impatient with his sightseeing to wait. He let her take control despite starting out this jaunt with his own pleasure in mind because in the end, they both won.

Far too quickly, she had them both gasping through a mutual, explosive orgasm. It took him by surprise, engulfing him, which made it that much more powerful.

He gathered her up and held her tight, loath to let go. After all, sex was the only normal part of their relationship. Why not spend as much time in bed as possible? Here he could pretend nothing had changed in their relationship and that the Back to Basics Plan was still about making sure he was included in doctor's appointments from now on.

He knew deep down that was a lie. But he couldn't deal with the truth.

"I have to go to work. It's Friday," she reminded him, though she didn't sound too thrilled about it. She sighed and pushed at his arms with very little strength. He didn't let go.

"Call in sick." He kissed her temple. "You're allowed to take time off, especially since you've probably already worked sixty hours this week."

She scowled. "I'm not an hourly employee. I never monitor my time like that. Fyra is my company that I built alongside my friends. I like my job."

"Okay." He held up his hands in mock surrender despite feeling anything but conciliatory. Now was not the time to push, obviously, even though part of the reason he'd come home a day early was to make sure she was taking care of herself. And not working too much.

So he'd let her think she'd won that round and help her climb from bed. As she padded across the room toward the bathroom, he called out, "I'll come by this morning and we can catch up on the FDA status."

She glanced over her shoulder. "Sure. I have an opening at eleven."

Excellent. That gave him time to devise a plan to get her out of the office for lunch. And if he played his cards right, she wouldn't be going back until Monday.

His wife needed rest and relaxation. It was his job to make sure she got that. The other stuff going on in their relationship could be ignored if he put his mind to it.

Eight

Melinda, Fyra's receptionist, smiled as Phillip strode through the glass doors of Alex's company.

"Mr. Edgewood, always a pleasure. I didn't know you were in town."

"Short notice," he allowed easily. "Alex penciled me in at eleven."

Melinda glanced at her computer screen, the corners of her mouth tilting down. "Oh, she must have gotten the time wrong. She's in a meeting with the people who run our accounting software."

"No problem." Phillip pasted on his Capitol Hill smile, the one he reserved for lobbyists and the media. "I'll wait in her office."

Cooling his heels in Alex's office gave Phillip plenty of time to think. And the FDA approval process didn't cross his mind once. There was some movement on that front, but concern for the health of his wife and babies trumped government bureaucracy. By the time said wife strolled through the door forty-five minutes later, he had his strategy laid out for how he would get her out of this place.

"Great timing," he said pleasantly as she eyed him warily. "I have reservations at the Crescent for lunch. We'll eat and talk about the status of the FDA application, and then we've been invited to the new children's hospital ribbon cutting this afternoon. We have just enough time to run by the house so you can change."

"Hello to you, too," she said with obvious sarcasm. "I have a protein bar for lunch that I brought from home and three meetings this afternoon. The ribbon cutting sounds great, but today is impossible."

Actually, he'd already convinced Melinda to rearrange Alex's schedule, and it had been far too easy to sway the receptionist to his way of thinking—namely that Alex needed the break—which told him his wife was definitely working entirely too much. But she clearly hadn't glanced at her calendar yet in order to notice her clear afternoon.

"We had an appointment that you blew off. You owe me." He raised his brows, driving the point home. He wasn't above layering on some guilt if it got her out of the office.

She sighed. "You're right. The meeting with the software people was critical since it's nearly quarter end, but I could have scheduled it another time. I didn't think you'd mind and took advantage of our relationship."

Well, that was laying it on a bit thick, but it worked in his favor, so he bit his tongue. "It's okay. I forgive you. As long as you agree to go to the ribbon cutting with me. That's one of the reasons we got married, right? So we could do things like that together."

"I'll get my purse."

Victory, Phillip. She even let Randy drive and settled into the town car without a peep about leaving her own car in the Fyra parking lot. There was a brief scuffle over Alex changing clothes, but Phillip smoothed over it with the very well-made point that the Crescent Hotel's restaurant had a strict dress code.

Once at home, Alex scowled and took the green Ralph Lauren from Phillip's outstretched hand. "I've never even seen this dress before."

"I bought it for you." Phillip twirled his finger in a get-on-with-it motion. "I'm dying to see it on you. It's the right size, isn't it?"

That must have been the correct way to play it because Alex threw it on the bed so she could slip off her jeans. A bonus Phillip hadn't expected—he was going to get to watch his wife dress.

As she slithered out of her shirt, his whole body reacted favorably to the sight of lush woman in nothing but a bra and panties. He thought seriously about blowing off his own plans for the day. What was wrong with playing hooky entirely from senator duties? When the mayor had called about the ribbon cutting, it had seemed like a perfect solution to Phillip's problem with Alex. She needed a break; the ribbon cutting was nothing more than a big party where he and his wife would be the guests of honor. It was a low-key event and he got to spend time with Alex. Win-win.

But then she pulled the dress over her head, and as it settled down around her breasts and hips, she twirled and struck a pose. "What do you think?"

His lungs felt like an elephant had just sat on them because he couldn't breathe. The brown fleck in her eye, the one that marked her so uniquely, stood out against the grass-green dress, and the hue complemented her pregnancy glow with unexpected flawlessness. She pulled the ponytail holder from her hair, letting it tumble down her back in a mass of loose waves.

"Gorgeous," he murmured. "We have to get out of here now before I undo all that."

She shot him a smug smile. "That good? You should buy me more clothes."

"I plan to," he growled. Lingerie, tiny silk robes, the works. "Later. Let's go eat before I lose my mind."

Laughing, she led the way to the car, and somehow, that had broken the mood, on her end at least. She chatted on the way to the restaurant, asking him questions about the FDA application. Since he'd been the one to bring it up— even though it had been a ploy to get himself into her office, so he could extract her—he obliged her with a status report, explaining that the FDA had scheduled a hearing a week from Monday.

It was a small measure of progress, he told her, but his mind wasn't on anything other than how quickly they could get through lunch and the party so he could be alone with his wife again.

Lunch was nearly as torturous.

If he'd have known buying Alex a dress would be so affecting, he might have picked something else. When he'd seen it in the shop window he hadn't hesitated, had just walked inside and had it shipped home. George had signed for the package and had the dress hung up in Alex's closet.

That was how things should work. Buy your wife a gift, and she wears it. Simple. It was anything but. Somehow the act of clothing her constantly reminded him of the act of unclothing her. He wanted to strip her out of the dress with his own two hands and watch as her luscious skin was revealed inch by inch. He wanted to kiss her and watch her face as he pushed into her again and again.

The dress was too distracting. His wife was too distracting.

Alex laughed at something he said, her face lighting up,

and he changed his mind. No. He needed to buy ten more dresses exactly like it. What was wrong with wanting his wife? Perfectly normal.

It just didn't feel normal or friendly or partner-y or whatever they were doing. It felt like…*more*.

And that was dangerous to his careful sense of propriety about their relationship. How could he stay true to Gina if he let himself feel all these *things* for his new wife?

He risked putting his hand against her back as they left the Crescent, guiding her toward the car as Randy sailed to the curb and stopped smoothly in the valet lane. Not because she needed help walking but because he wanted to touch her. But she ducked into the car too fast and he missed the feel of fabric stretched over her body.

The hospital parking lot was a madhouse, so Randy dropped them off in a side lot. They had to walk around to the front where the ribbon-cutting ceremony would be held, which gave Phillip exactly the opportunity he was looking for to put his arm around Alex again.

Throngs of people milled about in the clearing near the entrance. A scarlet ribbon blocked the sliding glass doors, emblazoned with Wharton Children's Hospital. Ceremonial shears the size of his desk stood on end against one of the posts, waiting for the hospital board and guest of honor.

Phillip had donated a lot of money to the hospital building fund and he was glad his schedule had allowed him to participate. Or rather, he was glad his wife's stubbornness had reared its head at the time that it had.

"There are a lot of people here," Alex muttered into his ear, leaning into his embrace a little deeper. A sure indicator that she was nervous.

"You'll be fine," he assured her with a light kiss to her temple that drew a small smile from her. Something pulled tight in his chest as she lifted her chin a touch to prolong the contact of his lips on her face. Such a small, brief moment. Why did it feel so massive?

A flash went off in his peripheral vision. Odds were good that the press had just captured that moment for all posterity. That should be a good thing. That was what they were here for. To schmooze and give photo ops, drum up support for Phillip's name and platform. All press was good press.

Except this time, it was intrusive. That moment with his wife hadn't been for public consumption and it infuriated him to have it tarnished. But his life was not his own, and neither was hers.

"Come on." He led her to the knot of suits near the entrance, most of whom comprised the hospital board.

He introduced Alex around and she shook hands demurely, opting to keep her comments minimal and largely of the noncommittal variety. Good. She was learning. Something pulled inside his chest again and he rubbed it with the flat of his hand. What the hell was going on in there?

The ceremony began and the board president took the stage to say a few words about the financial generosity of the Wharton family for whom the hospital was named and then thanked a few local businessmen who had also donated money, including Phillip.

"I didn't know you'd given money," Alex whispered and her breath warmed his ear. "This is a great cause. I'm proud to be the plus one standing next to you. Why didn't you tell me?"

"It never came up," he said, suddenly uncomfortable with the direction of the conversation. He'd inherited a vast amount of wealth. So what? "It's not a big deal. I give money to lots of stuff."

But the admiration and pride shining from her eyes said

she thought it *was* a big deal and that sharpened the strange ache in his chest. He carried it with him as the president of the hospital board called Phillip up to help him, along with four other board members, cut the ribbon. They posed for pictures and then cut as one group. Just like he'd done a dozen times before, except never with Alex watching him while she wore a dress he'd selected and a smile he'd elicited through a deed she found heroic.

The mayor's wife approached Alex and he was too far away to hear the conversation, but they shook hands, then chatted for a moment. The mayor's wife kept smiling and even laughed at one point. Not once did she get that bemused, cockeyed look on her face that so commonly appeared on people's faces after two seconds in his wife's company.

When Phillip finally sprang free of his duties, he cornered Alex. "What did the mayor's wife say to you?"

"That she had naked pictures of Channing Tatum on her phone and did I want to see them?" Alex snorted as he raised a brow. "What do you think she said? She introduced herself and apologized for missing the wedding."

Okay, he'd probably deserved that. "She seemed charmed. That's good."

"I'm trying, Phillip. Like we talked about. I want to be an asset to you or I wouldn't be here." Alex folded her hands in front of her, clearly more poised than he would have expected, and even that sat funny on his nerves.

A beep from Alex's handbag interrupted and she fished out her phone, read the message and glanced up to meet his gaze, her expression clouding. "The problem with our accounting software just got worse. The vendor is on-site trying to help and they need my guidance. Sorry. I have to cut this afternoon short."

Disappointment flooded the ache in his chest, drowning

it thoroughly. "Fyra can survive without you until Monday. I need you by my side."

Actually, he needed her for a whole lot more than that. The reality of it froze his tongue. He could do a ribbon cutting without her. He'd been solo for two years with no problem.

But that wasn't the issue. He'd wanted to go home with her after this. Lock the bedroom door and forget about the outside world. Just spend his weekend reveling in her body, her smile, the way she made him feel.

That wasn't what was supposed to be happening in their relationship. When had Alex become so critical and necessary?

Panic pounded in his breastbone and melded with disappointment he absolutely should not be feeling.

"Well, I can't stay. This is *your* job." She waved curtly at the milling ribbon-cutting attendees. "Not mine. I have to go resolve these issues or Fyra's quarter-end filing will be late."

He shrugged, hoping it had come off as nonchalant. "Your company isn't publicly traded. It's not like your stock will tank if you don't produce a financial statement."

Alex went still. "What's that supposed to mean? Because Fyra's a private company, I shouldn't worry about a little thing like quarterly numbers? I'm talking about *tax* filing. That's not optional unless you know of some IRS loophole I've been ignorant of all this time."

Arms crossed, she stared him down, and yeah, he heard himself acting like an ass but couldn't physically stop himself. Not with all the panic still racing through his veins over when and how Alex had become someone he didn't like being separated from. "You're working too hard. It's not good for the babies. Maybe you should think about taking a leave of absence. Think about that instead of your numbers."

"What are you saying?" she whispered. "That it's not okay with you if I work simply because I'm pregnant? That was never part of our deal."

"Neither were twins, Alex." His voice rose too loudly for his own comfort, so he pulled her to a more private area and tried to reel in his temper because none of this was about her working. It had everything to do with making sure she knew this marriage was about the babies. Nothing more. "No second chances. If you harm the babies through your own selfishness, how will that sit with you?"

That had been over the line. He started to apologize but she cut him off.

"Is that how you think of my career? As being selfish?"

Stricken, her eyes went wide and filled with unshed tears. The tears cooled his temper instantly. He'd hurt her with his asinine comments and inability to have a conversation simply because she'd dug too far under his skin. Which was his fault, not hers.

Nonetheless, he'd started this showdown. And his points were still valid.

"I'm not talking about giving up your career. Just take it easy until the babies are born and maybe then stay home for six months? I don't know, just thinking out loud."

It was a compromise. He'd like to say she should consider being a stay-at-home mom. Twins were a huge responsibility. Plus, he worried about her. She should be resting, not pushing herself to the point of exhaustion.

With Gina, this conversation never would have happened. His first wife had talked for hours upon hours about how she couldn't wait to be a mother, couldn't wait to raise their children. She'd had no job outside of being his wife, and he'd never realized how that had translated into making his life easier. He had no practice at resolving marital disagreements because Gina had never disagreed with him.

"Keep thinking," Alex shot back, and one tear spilled down her face. "I'm going to work. You do your thing and maybe I'll see you later. Don't worry about me. I was taking care of myself just fine before you came along. Which means I can call a taxi on my own, too."

With that, she flounced off as she angrily dashed the tear away, leaving Phillip with a burn in his chest, no plus one and no explanation for why he wanted to punch the wall. Or maybe he should just punch himself. It would probably hurt less than being responsible for making Alex cry.

Phillip slunk to his car, but instead of directing Randy to drive home, he asked to be taken to his grandfather's house. Max Edgewood was the only person on earth who would give Phillip a warm welcome no matter what. And honestly, he needed a friendly face right now.

Amelia, his grandfather's maid, answered the door the moment Phillip knocked. Randy had called ahead as he drove so Max would be expecting visitors. The older Phillip's grandfather grew, the less he got out of bed, but for some reason, he refused to receive visitors while laid up. So there was a process to get the elderly man dressed and into his wheelchair so he could be taken to the ground floor by elevator.

As expected, Max sat in the formal parlor with a wide smile on his face and an oxygen tank hooked to the back of his chair. "There's my favorite grandson."

"Last time I checked, I was your only grandson. You uncover a long-lost relative I don't know about?"

It was an old, beloved routine, but it warmed up the cold place in Phillip's gut that had formed when his wife stormed off. Because her husband had hurt her over his own conflicted emotions.

"Never," his grandfather announced imperiously. "In my day, we didn't lose track of our family, even without the benefit of Facebook and thingamajigs that beep and vibrate and who knows what all."

"Still not a fan of cell phones?" Phillip let his face fall in mock disappointment. "Too bad. I bought you one for your birthday."

"Well, that's a horse of a different color. A man cannot in good conscience refuse a thoughtful gift. Give it here." Max nodded and held out his hand.

"Ha. Your birthday isn't for two months. Don't you try to con your way into an early present because it won't work. But I might have something else…"

He drew it out as long as possible because he knew Max well and the man could not stand to be left hanging. He'd instantly become a dog fighting over a prized bone. It was one of the qualities that had made him such a great senator.

His grandfather scowled without any real heat. "Don't toy with me. I taught you those tricks, boy."

With a smile, Phillip handed over the ultrasound pictures he'd tucked into his wallet yesterday. Max glanced at them, then back up at Phillip quizzically. Then the light dawned. His eyes went wide as he stared at the pictures. "Two?" he whispered. "You're giving me two great-grandchildren?"

"Only because you're the best grandfather in the world," Phillip confirmed as Max laughed out loud, drawing the attention of Amelia and Nancy, his full-time nurse, both of whom rushed into the room to see what was happening.

"Look at this, ladies. I'm gonna be a great-grandpa times two."

Amelia and Nancy oohed and aahed over the ultrasound

photos, but you could only look at blobs for so long. They congratulated Phillip and drifted back to their posts.

"You should have brought your lovely new wife by," Max suggested and waggled his bushy brows. "I haven't even met her yet."

Guilt crowded into Phillip's chest, and there hadn't been that much room in the first place with all the other stuff going on inside. His grandfather couldn't travel and hadn't been able to make the wedding, and then Phillip had been so busy commuting back and forth before and after that he hadn't made the time.

All just excuses in the end and not the real reason. If anyone would see his marriage as a sham, it would be Max, and Phillip hadn't wanted to answer any pointed questions about the nature of the agreement between him and his wife. Not in front of the one person who would instantly clue in on how it *looked* like Phillip had moved on…but really hadn't.

"Next time," he said instead.

If there was a next time. The fight he'd just had with Alex came rushing back, and it must have registered on his face because Max narrowed his gaze far too shrewdly for someone with cataracts.

"Trouble in paradise already?"

Phillip scrubbed his face. "She's working twelve, fourteen hours a day. I don't think it's good for her or the babies, and I guess trying to talk to her about it was the wrong move. She got pretty upset and stormed off."

"Take it from me. I'm an old widower but marriage hasn't changed in sixty years. You're wrong, no matter what. Apologize and make it good," Max advised and then shushed Phillip as he started to speak. "No, really. You're wrong. Trust me."

"So, I'm supposed to be okay with the fact that she's working so much?" Phillip frowned. "I can't accept that."

"Oh, I didn't say I agreed with her. I said you're wrong. You can spin that with her however you want. You handled it wrong. You were wrong to upset her. You misunderstood the question and gave the wrong answer. Whatever works to make her feel like she's understood and being heard. That's what women really want."

Phillip raised a brow. "You never gave me that advice when I was married to Gina."

"Gina was a sweet lady and you were so in love with her." Max smiled craftily. "But you were her whole world. She didn't have a life outside of Phillip Edgewood, United States senator. This new marriage is not the same. You have to give more because Alexandra is older than Gina was when you married her. More set in her ways. Less pliable. You don't want a pliable woman anyway, son. You married this one because she's totally different from Gina. Admit it."

Yes.

Shock shut Phillip's mouth so he couldn't say it out loud, but he was pretty sure he didn't have to. Of course Alex wasn't anything like Gina, but he'd been so busy following the rules to keep his new wife at arm's length that he hadn't stopped to examine *why* he'd been so attracted to someone so unlike his first wife.

He'd like to claim he'd done it deliberately, so he could guarantee he'd never fall for Alex. But that was the reason he'd married her, not the reason he was so attracted to her. That, he couldn't control. At all. Alex made him feel things he'd never felt for any woman before, and being the mother of his children had a lot to do with it. He could pretend all day long that was all it was—a fondness for the woman bearing his twins. But that wasn't all it was. No amount of guilt or pretending could change that.

"How did you get to be so smart, anyway?"

"Don't be grouchy just because I'm right." Max put a soothing gnarled hand on Phillip's shoulder and paused as his voice dissolved into a phlegmy coughing fit. When he'd recovered, he asked, "Now, what's really going on? You didn't have a fight about her working too hard because I'm pretty sure a woman who founded her own company always works a lot of hours."

That was what he got for telling his grandfather so much detail about the woman he'd married. Phillip's shoulders slumped as he recalled that Alex had said something very similar. "Yeah. It's kind of a mess."

The whole story poured out before Phillip even registered opening his mouth. How he didn't want to be in love again. Too painful. Much easier to go into a marriage without expectations. He needed a wife. Alex hadn't wanted to get married but he'd talked her into it.

Maybe *guilted* her into it was a better description.

Max nodded here and there but didn't interrupt. When Phillip finished talking, his heart felt ten pounds lighter. Who would have thought confession would be so good for his soul?

"I thought for sure that a marriage based on a mutual agreement would work." Phillip stared at his wedding ring. White gold instead of yellow because he hadn't wanted it to be the same as the first one. "But I have no idea how to handle things with Alex. Did I make a mistake, Grandpa?"

Fear seized his lungs, and he couldn't breathe. If he had made a mistake, that meant he had to make it right. That meant losing Alex. And his babies. He couldn't.

Max worked his lips, his gaze distant and thoughtful. "Here's the thing, son. Marriage isn't about how much you love someone or what *you* need. It's about how much you're willing to give. How well you're meeting *her* needs. Doesn't matter why you got married. Only whether you're willing to do the work."

His grandfather's advice ringing in his ears, Phillip flashed back to all the events since Alex had announced she was pregnant. She hadn't wanted to get married. He'd convinced her. She hadn't wanted to be a politician's wife. He'd blown that off and told her she'd be great. She hadn't wanted to be alone in the house when he wasn't there. He'd tried to take away her one refuge—numbers.

She'd done all the hard work thus far.

All this time, he'd thought he was being unfair to Alex because he'd sworn to withhold love from her, and it had blinded him to all the other imbalances going on. Instead of throwing his weight around, he should be bowing and scraping and treating her like royalty. He had to fix things or he would lose his plus one due to his own idiocy. Make that his plus three.

He'd assumed the learning curve would be steeper for Alex because she'd never been married before. But he hadn't realized that it would be a totally different ball game for him too the second time. Because he'd married a different woman. For different reasons.

"What should I do?" Phillip murmured.

"You already know the answer to that." Max nodded once for emphasis and started coughing again.

Phillip had overtaxed his grandpa with his own foolishness. It was way past time to leave. And his grandfather was right. There was no mystery here. He had to admit he was wrong and start working as hard on his marriage as Alex was. Easy. Look how brilliant she'd been at the ribbon cutting. Had he even thanked her? He couldn't remember.

He stood and rubbed Max's shoulder. "I should go. I

need to talk to my wife and let you rest. Okay if I bring her by sometime?"

"Of course. How else would I get a chance to steal her away from you?"

Phillip grinned. "Ha. You can try, old man, but you will not succeed."

"Bring it on," Max called out as Phillip left, a new plan already forming in his mind.

Back to Basics had been a great start but he needed something bigger: the Give Back Plan, which included making sure Alex got what she needed in this relationship. As long as he stuck to the rules, he could afford to be a lot more emotionally supportive.

Nine

Alex pivoted, but her stomach didn't look any less flat from that angle than it had from the left side. The mirror had to be broken. When was she going to start showing? Three months pregnant was a third of the way there.

She wanted to see some physical change, some hint of the miracle going on inside. Something that would prove she hadn't done the babies any harm by continuing to nurture her career as well as the twins.

Because at least half the reason she was still upset about the fight with Phillip a day later had to do with guilt. What if he was right? What if something terrible happened because she refused to listen to him? Morning sickness was a giant flashing warning, her body's way of saying *slow down*. And she hadn't been heeding the message.

At least all her clothes still fit. Shopping was not high on her list of pleasurable activities and she was kind of banking on Trinity and Cass picking out all her maternity clothes when the time came.

She glanced up as Phillip appeared in the mirror behind her.

"Ready to go?" he asked.

He'd come home last night with a dozen roses and a sweet apology. She'd accepted both. But hadn't forgiven or forgotten the reason they'd had a fight. Mostly because she'd got exactly what she deserved after filling in the *if only* blank. She'd let herself start to hope, just a tiny bit and *bam*…they'd got into an argument because she'd forgotten the rules. They were partners, not lovers who supported each other no matter what. No second chances, period, end of story. Hoping for something more? That had been the biggest in a long line of mistakes.

No more mistakes. If she screwed up, her kids would be fatherless, just like she'd been. That was not happening. This marriage was strictly designed to ensure her family didn't suffer because of her own selfishness.

So things between her and Phillip were…strained, for lack of a better word. Of course, they hadn't been married but a little over a week. Maybe this was normal for them.

"As ready as I'll ever be," she allowed and slicked on a coating of Harper's Crushed Blush lipstick, which she'd had for a year without using it all.

They'd been invited to a party at Phillip's parents' house, which she sorely did not want to attend but couldn't think of a good excuse for skipping. The question of her working through her pregnancy had not been broached again, but neither was it resolved, and the last thing she wanted to do was spend time faking her enthusiasm for the Edgewood clan.

But this was her role in the marriage. It was a fair trade for giving her babies a father. She just wished she didn't have to keep reminding herself that she was getting a good deal out of this.

Phillip had abracadabra-ed another dress from her closet that she'd never seen, and part of her wanted to hate it. But she didn't. It was a beautiful off-white wrap dress with a long skirt that reminded her of something Marilyn Monroe would wear.

She put it on. It fit. She looked spectacular in it. What was there to hate?

But she couldn't help feeling like a trophy wife. *Her.* Alexandra Meer…er, Edgewood. Her husband wanted to trot her out like a show pony, provided she had the right saddle. Coupled with everything else, especially the seesaw of emotions she constantly rode, it was too much.

They drove to the party in silence, though Phillip kept shooting her glances like he wanted to say something but wasn't sure how it would be received. Smart man.

The senior Edgewoods lived a short distance away in a newer part of Preston Hollow. New being relative; Phillip's house had been built in 1938. The Edgewoods' sprawling property rivaled their son's in elegance and beauty but clearly had a more modern design.

Randy opened the door and the Edgewoods' butler helped Alex from the car. Phillip put his hand on her back to escort her up the stairs. It was a simple gesture, but his touch burned through her.

Okay, that might be the sole physical response she couldn't chalk up to anything more than the pregnancy. Why did her body respond so quickly and ferociously when all Phillip had done was absently touch her? It was maddening.

The party was in full swing. People thronged the expansive grounds at the rear of the Edgewood property, all seemingly in a festive mood.

Alex pasted on a smile and greeted people she vaguely remembered from the wedding. She'd been so sick that day. She'd barely registered much of anything, let alone people's names.

Today, the swirl in her stomach had everything to do with uncertainty and a strong desire to not say anything that would raise eyebrows. Mostly that meant she had to keep her mouth shut and let Phillip do all the talking. Easy. He was a born charmer.

To her shock, he didn't park in the middle of a group and start chatting as he usually did. With barely a nod to those who called out to him, Phillip swept her past the knots of people and ushered her straight to a nearly empty gazebo overlooking the pool, pointing her to a wicker love seat. "This is your spot. Relax and I'll bring you a drink. Ginger ale?"

"Um...sure?" A bit off-kilter, she watched him thread back to the bar set up on the south end of the pool and accept a clear plastic cup from the uniformed bartender.

Phillip didn't stop to talk to one single person as he rushed her drink to her waiting hand.

"What else can I get you? Something to eat?" he asked.

"What's going on?" she blurted out. "Why are we here if you're not going to work the crowd?"

He sat on the love seat next to her, his gaze riveted to her face and not scanning the crowd for someone he needed to speak to. She was it, and oh, how she felt it deep inside.

"Because it's a party and I thought it was important that we have fun. Together. We don't do that."

"No, not as a rule." Or rather, because of the rules. They didn't have a relationship where they had *fun*. Did they? "Out of sheer curiosity, what would be the definition of *fun*?"

He smiled, and it washed over her with unexpected force. Like it had the night of another party. "A drink. Maybe I tell you a joke and you laugh. We talk about our favorite TV shows from when we were in third grade and perhaps a few interesting people happen by who join in on the conversation. Maybe we'll all weigh in on whether our parents let us watch *Blossom* or thought we were too young."

She couldn't help it. The laugh came out on its own.

"Hey," he protested. "I didn't tell you the joke yet."

"I was like seven when *Blossom* went off the air. I only cared about dolls and ponies and kitty cats, if I recall."

His grin widened and she forgot about the rest of the party. "Then you were definitely too young. Our kids won't be allowed to watch anything questionable until they turn twenty-one."

Our kids. It had such an intimate ring to it. She wanted to gather the feeling close and hold on to it. And that was enough to spring her guard back into place. "Really, you don't have to hang out with me. You should go network."

He waved off her comment. "I can do that anytime. I have to go back to Washington Sunday night and I want to spend time with you while I can."

Tenderness spread through his expression, and that was so lovely, she forgot why she wasn't supposed to let her heart squish when he looked at her.

A noise behind her alerted her to the presence of someone else, and reluctantly, she tore her gaze from her husband to see his mother clambering up the steps to the gazebo.

"Here's where you've spirited off my daughter-in-law to," Mrs. Edgewood exclaimed and swatted her son on the arm as she sank into the adjacent wicker armchair. "Whew, I was starting to think I'd never sit down. Thank you for picking such a great place to hide."

Guilt reared its ugly head, driving Alex to protest. "Oh, we're not hid—"

"You're welcome," Phillip interjected smoothly over

Alex's hasty response. "This is the best seat in the house for people watching."

Alex gave him the side-eye. Had he just admitted to his mother that he was avoiding people at his mother's own party? That was the kind of faux pas Alex usually made and had sworn to never make again.

But his mother laughed. "You used to come here all the time during parties when you were younger, Phillip. Remember? The adult ones you weren't invited to because they went on past your bedtime. You didn't think I knew, but Nana always kept me in the loop."

"Nana was my nanny," Phillip explained as an aside to Alex, still grinning fondly at his mother. "She had a real name but I couldn't pronounce it, so she was Nana until the day she left our employ. Little did I know she was a big tattletale about my nocturnal activities."

"Siobhan," Mrs. Edgewood supplied easily. "I could say it fine, but forget spelling it. Oh, she was a dear thing. We tag-teamed everything, from scraped knees to driving you to and from St. Mark's. His school," she explained to Alex.

Fascinated, Alex watched the exchange between Phillip and his mom. They had a bond that reminded her of the closeness she shared with her own mother, but different. Sure, Alex loved her mom, but their relationship had a lot of other things bound up in it: guilt and shame for the things she'd put her mother through. A sense of obligation. Her mother didn't have anyone else, had never remarried or even dated much after Alex's father left, so Alex was all she had.

And her mother had been instrumental in pulling Alex from the pit of self-destruction. She'd probably be dead or in jail right now without her mother. It made sense that Alex would remain mindful of the debt she owed.

The interaction between Phillip and his mother was totally different. They loved each other for no other reason than by virtue of being family. Not due to any rules or obligation. Just because. You could see it in their expressions, in the relaxed way they were with each other, in the tones of their voices.

Love didn't look like that in Alex's world. Never had. Her own father had left their family without a backward glance. So was it any wonder she'd never believed love existed?

Or had that belief been something she'd invented to avoid the question of *why* no one loved her like that?

"Alex, when you're ready to hire a nanny, if you want my help interviewing you just let me know." Mrs. Edgewood patted Alex's arm to punctuate that statement.

Stunned, Alex stared at Phillip's mother. Nanny? She hadn't even thought that far ahead, but of course she would need one. It wasn't like she could work sixty or seventy hours a week and raise two babies, especially not with a husband who commuted back and forth to Washington.

"That's very kind, Mrs. Edgewood."

"Oh, please don't call me Mrs. Edgewood. That just aged me twenty years. And I didn't need any help getting older." She shook her head with a laugh. "I'm Connie and we're family."

Tears pricked at Alex's eyes. Stupid pregnancy hormones. Why would Mrs. Edgewood say something like that? Alex wasn't family, not really. Not the kind she'd meant, like someone you loved for no reason other than because you wanted to. Her son certainly didn't.

But obviously he had the capacity for it. He'd loved Gina. Was there something fundamentally wrong with Alex that caused people to shy away from loving her?

A tear worked loose and slid down her face. Mortified, she swiped at it and then shrugged. It wasn't like she could hide it from the woman watching her so closely. "Thank you, Connie. I think that's the nicest thing anyone's said to me in a long time."

"Then you're hanging out with the wrong people." Glaring at her son with pointed barbs as if to include him in the category of *wrong people*, Connie smoothed a hand over Alex's shoulder. "You're the only daughter I've got. Let's make it count."

Oh, wow. That had not been anything like the reception she'd been braced for. There was an authenticity implied in the woman's statement that Alex craved all at once. Her relationship with Phillip might not be based on love but the one with Connie could be. There were no rules about that. If she wanted advice about hiring a nanny, who better to ask than a woman who'd married a politician, the same as Alex had?

They could be friends in an otherwise confusing Edgewood world. Somehow, the simple sentiment of being labeled Connie's daughter enclosed Alex in a big bubble of belonging, and now that she was inside it, she couldn't stand for it to burst.

"Okay." Alex nodded and another tear splashed to her lap. When had she started wanting so much more than rules to live by? Rules were the only thing that made sense and never changed. They kept you safe and free from consequences.

When had she started wanting to be loved?

Phillip's arm came around Alex and he pulled her close in wordless comfort. His touch warmed her, and it had nothing to do with sex. The moment swelled through her, fueled by the emotions already in play.

"You should be saying nice things to your wife all the time," his mother scolded. "Alex is the mother of your children. That automatically makes her worthy of being showered with all sorts of pretty words."

"I agree," Phillip said wryly. "But none of the stuff I'd like to say is fit for mixed company."

"Well, then, I'll leave you to your pillow talk." His mother didn't even blush, a trick Alex would like to learn because *her* cheeks had certainly prickled with heat at the blatant sexual innuendo. Connie stood and smiled at Alex. "Thank you for bringing light back into my son's life. His father and I worried he'd never get to this point after Gina passed. You're more of a blessing than you could ever know."

Connie sailed out of the gazebo, leaving Alex in a big puddle of confusion about what had just happened. Had she done that—brought some cheer into the life of a widower? Somehow she hadn't thought of him as grieving. And as revelations went, it was rather huge.

"Sorry, she didn't mean to make you uncomfortable."

Alex blinked and met Phillip's gaze. A warm breeze filtered through the gazebo, bringing with it the barest hint of honeysuckle and a clarity she hadn't realized she'd needed.

"She didn't. She's a lovely person." Her mind whirling furiously, Alex settled deeper into Phillip's embrace. "Did she make *you* uncomfortable? You don't talk about Gina much."

Bingo. Phillip shifted as if he couldn't find the right position. "Not much to talk about. She's gone."

He *was* uncomfortable talking about Gina. But if he didn't talk about her, how was he ever supposed to move past his feelings for her?

"But you loved her. That's a big, beautiful thing worth honoring."

At that, he full-out froze. Sounds of the party drifted through the sudden stillness and Alex had half a mind to quit while she was ahead. This was exactly the kind of foot in mouth she should be avoiding. But something about the way he'd talked to his mother, the relationship they had, made her ache. Physical needs she knew all about slaking. This man had a talent for it, and she had a pretty good handle on how to reciprocate. But what about emotional needs? His *and* hers? Why wasn't fulfilling those part of their deal?

Or was the real problem that neither of them knew what their emotional needs were? What if she could take this opportunity to find out and didn't?

She went for broke. "I've never been in love. What's it like?"

Phillip exhaled, and with it, some of the tension eased. "A miracle. A song that your soul can't stop singing. Energy. Light. Motivation. When you have it, things you never thought possible become achievable."

Transfixed, Alex listened to her husband express the poetry of his heart and her own twisted. The wrenching in her chest was equal parts awe and pain, like she'd glimpsed heaven only to have angry storm clouds race across the opening in the sky.

Because what he'd just described was what love meant to Phillip. Now that she'd heard it, experienced it in watching the way he interacted with his mother, she wanted it for herself. She wanted Phillip to believe he could have that again. That they could achieve it together, with each other.

And that was against the rules.

Alex bit her lip and held back additional tears. Barely. "No wonder you don't think you'll find that again. It sounds like a once-in-a-lifetime deal."

Which didn't necessarily mean that it was. There were no rules when it came to things of the heart. That was why she shied away from them so quickly. But this time, she didn't want to.

He nodded, surprise dawning in his expression. "You give me a lot of grace. I appreciate that. I keep expecting you to make demands of me that I can't fulfill and you never do. I've made some mistakes due to that and I'm sorry. I'm trying to stop operating on false assumptions."

He meant their fight about her working too hard. And the distance. All smoke screens to keep her from expecting too much. Because he didn't think he had any more to give than what he'd laid out at the beginning of their relationship.

And finally, she understood his emotional need in this relationship—to become a believer in second chances. Who better to help him learn that than someone who understood the power and mercy of being granted a do-over?

She carried the explosive secret with her for the remainder of the weekend.

When they got home from the party, where Phillip had done exactly as he said and spent the entire time with Alex having fun, he didn't disappear, mentally or physically.

They watched a movie on the giant theater screen in the media room and Phillip held her hand through the whole thing, except for the five minutes he left to get her a drink. They slept in the same bed, wrapped around each other like lovers. Because they were.

Just not yet the kind she'd started to believe—and hope—might be possible.

At breakfast Sunday morning, Phillip looked up from his English muffins, jam and scrambled eggs with a bittersweet smile. "I hate that I have to go back to Washington tonight."

"It's not ideal," she agreed. "I was hoping to get to a

point where I could come with you, but this week is impossible with quarter end. I have meetings all week."

"Speaking of which, a week from tomorrow, there's going to be a preliminary hearing about your FDA application. In Washington. I was planning to cover it for you."

"That would be great." She asked him a few questions about the process so she could report back to the other ladies in Fyra's C-suite about the next steps, which Phillip answered easily and thoroughly. Fyra had been truly blessed by his help.

He forked up a bite of eggs and chewed thoughtfully, his gaze on her. "We've known each other for a while now, and I don't think I've ever asked why cosmetics."

The question was so out of left field she had to take a minute to figure out what he was talking about. "You mean why did Cass, Trinity, Harper and I open shop to sell mascara instead of something else?"

"Yeah. I knew I wanted to be a senator by the time I was a senior in high school. And really for me, it was more of a decision on whether I wanted to go to the House or the Senate, not whether I'd go into politics at all. You had the whole world at your feet and chose mascara. I'm curious why."

She could lie. She did it all the time. But something about the way he asked, with no judgment, just a man curious about his wife's thoughts, made her want to answer honestly. If she hoped to reverse Phillip's stance on second chances, what better way to accomplish that goal than to tell the story of how she'd got hers?

"Cosmetics is their thing. I'm just along for the ride," she admitted, and the earth didn't crack open at her feet, so she went on. "I never planned to go to college. I wanted to have fun and hang out with my friends. Who were a boatload of trouble, but they were mine. You know? They listened to me and cared about me in the midst of my parents' painful divorce."

He nodded, but didn't interrupt.

"The first time we got arrested, they let us go with a warning. We thought we were invincible and did a lot of things we shouldn't have—drugs, shoplifting, graffiti. You name it, we did it."

It was a bland recitation of facts, but the anguish she still felt sometimes about her past came out in her voice. The concern painting her husband's face wasn't the revulsion she deserved.

"You needed your family and they weren't there," he said simply. "So you found a new one."

"Yeah. Then the music stopped when I was fifteen. I finally got the attention of someone who saw the train wreck about to happen and knew exactly how to fix it. Judge Miller. She was compassionate, just and really cared about her job."

Alex had realized all of this in hindsight, of course. At the time, she'd been disrespectful, mad about being caught and not about to let anyone know how scared she'd been. Judge Miller had told Alex she couldn't let her ruin her own life. The first of many second chances. Alex had quickly embraced them for the miracles they'd been.

And according to Phillip, *love* was a miracle. Maybe she'd been the recipient of more love than she'd realized over the years. The concept didn't feel so foreign all at once.

"How did she fix it?" Phillip had forgotten about his breakfast and sat with his attention squarely on Alex.

"After she sentenced me, she called me and my mother into her chambers and gave my mother the talking-to of her life. Said she was the one who could change things for me, and Judge Miller was going to hold her accountable for my probation. That was a turning point."

Her mother had taken that advice to heart, got Alex into a rehab program that actually worked and applied for every scholarship she thought her daughter had a marginal chance of receiving. With a lot of hard work, Alex had got her grades up enough to be accepted to the University of Texas.

She told Phillip about walking into freshman algebra, her first class as a college student, and sitting next to a friendly redhead who had knocked her pencil to the floor four times in fifteen minutes. Each time, Alex had picked it up with a smile of commiseration. Her own nerves had been strung tight, too.

By the end of the hour, Alex had known her classmate's name was Harper, that they shared a decided social awkwardness and that Harper had hoped to be a chemist when she grew up. Since Alex had had no clue what she'd wanted to be the following day, let alone in the future, and because she'd had a lack of friends without criminal records, Harper had seemed like someone from another planet.

A bit starstruck, Alex had expended monumental effort to match her new friend's over-the-top math skills. But it wasn't until the professor asked her to tutor another student that Alex had understood she possessed an unusual aptitude for numbers.

"The other student? It was Cass," Alex finished and had to swallow the sudden lump in her throat. "She was such a beautiful person. Still is. She believed in me from the very beginning. When she introduced me to Trinity, the first thing she said was 'I found our finance guru.' *Me.* Alex Meer, fresh from Podunk, Texas, and barely clear of my probation period. I never would have majored in finance without Cass. I never would have realized I liked numbers if I hadn't sat next to Harper that first day."

"That's a great story." Phillip squeezed her hand.

She hadn't even registered him taking it into his, but the silent comfort soothed the emotional smashup going on inside. "That's why I can't just quit. Cosmetics mean nothing to me, but friendship? That's everything. I would paint my body with mascara brushes if one of my partners asked me to."

"I see." He went quiet for a moment. "No wonder you got so angry with me when I mentioned it."

The fact that he got that squeezed her heart harder than he'd squeezed her hand. How did he affect her so much with simple words? Probably because she'd started to glimpse what could be possible between them and every moment in his presence reinforced it. She *wanted* to be affected. The emotional highs were addictive. Necessary. Wonderful.

"I didn't deserve a second chance, but I definitely believe in them." Let him do what he wanted to with that.

"I'm starting to get the point." With that cryptic comment, he kissed her fingertips and wandered down her arm to her elbow with so much serious intent that finishing breakfast became the last thing on either of their minds.

By the time he left that night, she hadn't got any closer to figuring out how to take their relationship to the next level. Or what that would even look like. Quandaries of the heart were not logical, and she was the last person who should be attempting to unravel this.

But comments like *I'm starting to get the point* gave her hope. Phillip had loved Gina so much. Maybe it was clouding his judgment about whether it could happen again. Lightning might not strike the same place twice, but who stood around in the exact same place waiting for it?

What had he said at the party? *Things you never thought possible become achievable.* She totally understood that now. Because she was pretty sure she was falling for her husband. That was so huge a revelation, it rendered her mute. And made the long week without Phillip seem that much longer.

On Monday, Melinda called her to the front desk because a dozen roses had just been delivered with Alex's name on them. Entranced, she rushed to the reception area to claim her vase. The note inside read: "One bouquet to commemorate our wedding day. —Phillip"

It was so sweet and surprising, she floated through the rest of the day.

On Tuesday, she received another delivery. Two dozen stargazer lilies with a note: "Two bouquets in honor of our twin babies. —Phillip"

She stared at the bouquets on her desk for a solid hour instead of focusing on the quarterly reports she needed to absorb before a meeting that afternoon. Phillip was obviously thinking about her. Missing her, maybe, like she was missing him. Their big house seemed so empty without him in it. Like her heart. She yearned to fill it with Phillip.

Perhaps he wanted to fill her heart and she just needed to let him.

On Wednesday, the reception area nearly burst at the seams as the entire office came to see what Phillip had sent. Three dozen larkspurs with a note: "Three bouquets. One for each month you've carried my children in your womb. —Phillip"

That one drew tears from her and at least half of the onlookers. She got it now. He was grateful for his children and wanted her to know, that was all. She'd never received flowers from anyone before and three in a row was something special. But she couldn't help wishing the flowers had been sent for more personal reasons.

Thursday, it was four dozen dendrobium orchids. The

note: "Four. That's how many orgasms I gave you last weekend. —Phillip"

No one in the reception area got to read that note and she blushed the rest of the day. Had the flower delivery people read it? Surely not. Next time, she'd be more careful what she wished for. But still. The flowers weren't just about the babies, like she'd convinced herself, strictly to avoid being disappointed. So what *were* they about?

On Friday, five dozen tulips in orange, red and yellow made the reception area look like the sun had burst open all over Fyra. The note read: "Five days I've had to wait to see you again. It's too many. —Phillip"

Something sharp and sweet spiked through her. Was all of this her husband's subtle way of saying his feelings were changing, as well? He was a rule follower, too. It was one of the many things they had in common. Maybe he was waiting for her to make the first move, in case she wasn't on board with coloring outside the lines. How could she find out?

Ask him, of course. But what if she turned out to be wrong? She was flying blind and terrified of messing up.

If she wanted something more than just being friends and partners with Phillip, she had to take that leap. They'd agreed divorce was off the table, so there was no reason to fear the consequences.

Last week, he'd come home to her. This time, she'd go to him. On the surface, she could pretend she'd elected to attend the FDA hearing on Monday in person. But in reality, for the first time since her youth, Alex was planning to break the rules.

Ten

Last week, Phillip had jetted home without even stopping by his condo. By five o'clock on Friday, he was starting to think that sounded like an even better idea this week.

Opposition to the bill he was cosponsoring with Senator Galindo had been fierce, and she and Phillip had spent the past week duking it out side by side on the Senate floor. The bill had failed to even make it to a vote.

He wanted to go home to Dallas and sink into Alex for reasons he was too tired to examine. She'd make it all go away with her smile and her pretty hair that felt like silk against his fingers. But the three-hour flight loomed, long and boring and so not what he wanted to do, and he hadn't even left Capitol Hill yet.

This commuting back and forth arrangement had serious holes in it. But he and Alex were stuck in it for the time being. He was trying to be patient with all of the complexities of their relationship, but something had to give.

A bit disgusted with the world in general, he trudged to his car and let Randy drive him back to the condo so he could dump his briefcase at least. But when he walked in the door, the light in the kitchen was on. Instantly on guard, he pulled out his phone to call 911…when Alex emerged from the bedroom.

Alex. Wearing a silk robe and a smile. And nothing else. He hoped.

The phone dropped from his nerveless fingers. "What—"

"Shh. I wanted to surprise you. Consider it an in-person thank-you for the flowers."

She advanced to the spot where he'd become rooted to the floor and he couldn't do anything other than watch the sexy sashay. He didn't want to do anything else on earth besides that.

"Yeah?" he croaked. "Found the robe I bought you, did you?"

He swallowed the question as she took hold of his tie, pulling on it sharply to bring his mouth to hers.

And then his brain dissolved as his wife devoured him, kissing him with a burst of pent-up passion. Or maybe that was his own kettle hitting full boil and whistling for all it was worth. Because holy hell, her tongue slicked along his, hot and strong and determined to unravel him in one shot.

It was working.

His wife had flown to Washington. To be with him. He'd reached out, tried to change the dynamic between them so they could get their relationship on even ground, and she'd reached back. Wow, had she reached back.

He should be the one doing the thanking. She was exactly what he'd needed, exactly what he'd wanted. All his fantasies wrapped up in an amazing package that he didn't have to wait one second to enjoy. It was like she'd read his mind.

His heart shattered and knit back together again instantly. He should probably care more about the ramifications of that.

She backed him up against one of the pillars separating the family room and the kitchen. His shoulder blades hit it a moment before her lush breasts smashed against his torso. He groaned. Even through his suit jacket he could feel her hard nipples. Lust rocketed through him, hardening everything in its path, and she purred her approval as her hands examined every inch of it.

"Too many clothes," she muttered and yanked off his suit jacket, popping a button in her haste. Enthusiastically, he helped her get the rest off and then the silk of her robe brushed across his skin, shooting sparks of sensation far and wide.

"Not you," he murmured hoarsely. "You're wearing exactly the right amount."

Provided she was naked under that robe...and lo and behold, she was. His palms cupped her bare rear and shoved, grinding her against his erection.

More. Now. Fast.

His mouth hot on hers again, he picked her up and stumbled to the kitchen...or the living room...or at least something that had a surface at waist height, and set her down. Because he wanted to use his hands and couldn't hold her up at the same time.

Falling into her, he gathered up the edges of the robe and pulled them wide, baring her breasts to his hungry gaze. Licking one nipple into his mouth, he sucked as his hands circled her stomach, thighs and then finally honed in on the sweet spot, pulling a hard gasp from her as he pushed into her slick center with two fingers, then three.

Not enough. He wanted to feel everything.

Centering her, he plunged in to the hilt and a gasp burst

from his own throat. Perfection. She rolled her hips, drawing him deeper, urging him on with little cries that inflamed his thrusts until they both came in a rush, pulsing in tandem. His knees nearly gave out from the force of his release.

And then he just held on to her, still deep inside, still caught up in the wash of pleasure. He closed his eyes and let his head rest on hers as something warm burst open in his chest.

He knew exactly what it was. Something that wasn't supposed to be there but had been for a while. Something wholly encompassing that was so much stronger in this moment after making love to his wife.

Where had that *come* from?

The black box inside had been locked up for so long. Exactly the way he'd wanted it. No emotions meant no pain.

Of course he cared about Alex. She was carrying his children. They were married. That warmth was only natural, he assured himself with something akin to panic.

She sighed against his neck, her legs clamped tight around his waist in the midst of an encounter that had only happened because she'd cut her workday short so she could fly three hours to see him. It was a huge concession, one that wasn't lost on him, and the warmth he'd been trying to deny spread to his heart, filling him.

Leftover reaction from the sex. Which had been so unbelievable. That was all this was. Of course he'd have some residual heat from that; it had been hot.

Relief settled over him. After the conversation with his grandfather, he'd known he had to do something to change his relationship with Alex or he risked losing what he'd perceived to be a tenuous hold on Alex and his babies. Looked like it had worked.

"You're welcome," he murmured when he could speak through all the *stuff* going on inside. "For the flowers."

It had been a spontaneous thought born of a long night alone last Sunday. He'd lain in bed remembering their weekend together and had wanted to do something to let her know he missed her. Part of the hard work Max had entreated him to take on, but it hadn't felt like work.

"The notes were the best part," she whispered into his ear and her legs tightened around him, increasing the contact between their bodies. "They were like a secret message."

"Oh?"

"Yeah. You picked out the most important highlights of our relationship and dedicated a note to each one. We're married. Having a family together. We can't keep our hands off each other because we've always been hot for one another." She ticked off each point against his shoulder. "And we like being with each other. Sharing a life. So much so that we miss each other. Marriage is so much better than what we thought it was going to be. That's what you meant. Right?"

Hearing it all encapsulated like that—no, that wasn't at all what he'd intended but he liked her points. What she'd said was exactly how he felt. Maybe he had subconsciously wanted to pay tribute to what was great about where they'd ended up.

"Yeah, sure. You're onto me."

Actually, it wasn't perhaps as subconscious as he'd pretended. The notes were also parameters. They carefully defined the box he'd put around their relationship. *These are the things our relationship is. The omissions are the things our relationship is not.*

It was inside of those parameters where he felt safest. Nothing bad would happen if they just stuck to the agreement. No emotional commitment meant no guilt, and it meant he'd never have to relive those hours and days after losing the most important thing in his life. And the fact that Alex got that was amazing. Wonderful. Miraculous.

The warmth in his chest started to bother him. He couldn't exactly claim to still be in the throes of post-orgasm. What was he doing still engaged with her like this? It was dangerous.

Alex cupped his face with her palms and kissed him sweetly, then drew back to bowl him over with a misty smile. Shiny moisture gathered in the corners of her eyes. "That's great. Because I'm falling for you, too."

"You're…what?" His voice cracked. "*Falling? For me? Too?*"

Parroting her words did not cause them to magically become coherent. While he'd been busy lying to himself about what was happening on his side of the fence, it had never occurred to him that *she'd* be veering from the rules.

She cocked her head, her smile slipping a touch. "Well… yeah. That's what we're talking about. Right? Our feelings toward each other are growing stronger. Deeper. The agreement didn't cover what would happen if we fell in love. So what do we do with that?"

Yes, of course their feelings were deeper than they had been. They were living together, married—but not *in love*. Okay, sometimes he couldn't sleep when she wasn't there. Sometimes his heart got a little warm when he looked at her. So what? That wasn't the same as what she was talking about.

Or was she seeing something he hadn't dared admit, even to himself?

"We're not…" His throat tightened, almost strangling him as he shut his eyes, willing back the panic clawing through his gut. "The agreement didn't cover it because it's not happening."

Crush it now. Don't let anything change.

The rules were in place for a reason; so she didn't expect something he was unwilling to give. But it was too late to backpedal. Even he could see that as she flinched.

Caution clouded her expression. "Not happening? You can't tell me how I feel, Phillip. Nor can you lie away your own feelings."

This was really, truly happening. They were having a conversation about the very thing he'd taken so many pains to avoid. The conflict inside between the guilt over his faithlessness toward Gina and the future he could have with Alex roared to life, clawing through him with metal teeth.

Wrenching away from her, he went in search of his clothes. He didn't want to have this conversation at all, let alone while naked.

She followed him into the living area, drawing her robe closed and belting the sash. She clearly didn't realize he'd been seeking distance. She perched on the edge of a wing-back chair flanking the fireplace. Quickly, he threw on his shirt and pants but couldn't find the left leg hole until he sat on the couch. Dazed, he stared at the carpet, the giraffe-stone fireplace, anywhere but at his wife as he told her what she needed to hear.

"I'm not lying away my feelings," he insisted. He despised politicians who lied as a matter of course. His honesty had always been one of his trademarks; that was the reason he was in this marriage, because he hadn't wanted to mislead his constituents. "I don't mean that I'm trying to will it away. I mean it's not on the table. It's not an option."

Which was true but wasn't necessarily the same as the

whole truth, and that was something he wasn't willing to offer. Because the way he felt about Alex had veered into dangerous territory a long time ago. And he'd tried—unsuccessfully—to mitigate those circumstances.

His heart belonged to Gina and no other woman could ever breach that wall. No other woman could be allowed inside. It wasn't fair to anyone, but it was the way things were.

It rang a little less true than it had in the past. And that was the worst revelation of all. If he allowed himself to love Alex, he'd be allowing himself the possibility of being emotionally destroyed all over again. He couldn't do it.

He was hurting her. The pain etched into her face nearly undid him. This was the reason he'd avoided women who wanted a love match. What had happened to his perfect, loveless marriage? Dumb question—emotions had happened to it. His and hers, effectively killing their agreement. It was a disaster.

Everything was falling apart and he didn't have a clue how to save it.

"You say it's not an option," Alex countered far more calmly than the tango in her stomach should have allowed. "But one of your points about getting married was that you wanted our children to grow up in a home like the one you had."

This was not going like she'd envisioned. Phillip hadn't fallen into her arms and thanked her for reading between the lines of his notes. In fact, if anything, she'd say they were headed in the opposite direction. His slightly panicked expression and superquick donning of his clothes had a lot to do with that impression.

The magic she'd thought had sparked between them in

the kitchen had thoroughly fizzled. Why had she thought baring her soul would be a good idea?

"Yeah. It is one of the reasons." Even his tone of voice had flattened out.

Pandora's box had been opened, and though she'd like nothing more than to slam the lid closed, she forced out the words. Do-or-die time. If she wanted more, she had to reach out. If she wanted to be loved, she had to say so.

"Your parents are very much in love, even now. Anyone can see that. Maybe that's part of the equation. Love is what creates that environment for kids. So what if we keep fast to the agreement and that turns out to be worse for our children? Why not explore all the options?"

There it was. Her best argument for taking their relationship to places they'd never expected. The logic was sound. If there was any chance of getting her husband on board with the possibility of a love match, logic was it. She held her breath.

"It's not an option," he repeated as his expression closed in. "We talked about this. You know what I'm willing to give and what I'm not."

Because his first wife was such a paragon that Alex couldn't measure up. Being the mother of his children didn't give her any special rights to his heart. He'd been more than clear about that all along.

Bitterness rose up in her throat. "Gina is gone, Phillip. You have to get over her and live your life for you and your children."

He froze, and his entire demeanor iced over. "That's not your call."

His tone cut through her, heightening the sick wave of panic and pain that had been brewing since she first admitted she was falling for him and he didn't say it back.

She'd screwed up. She never should have said anything. That was what she got for trying to get out of her comfort zone. For daring to believe that she'd found someone who would love her madly, passionately, like Phillip had loved Gina. She'd really thought… Obviously, she'd imagined Phillip had developed any sort of feelings toward her other than gratitude. But the notes had been so sweet and the way he looked at her sometimes… Her heart lurched as she stared at his implacable expression.

No. This was not her fault. Her feelings had changed and he didn't get to dictate that.

She wanted the husband she'd convinced herself he was becoming. It wasn't what they'd talked about or what she'd thought would happen, but that didn't make it any less valid. And she'd fight for what she hoped could be the outcome of this argument. "Well, the agreement's not working for me anymore. That *is* my call."

Frowning, he eyed her. "What are you saying?"

"I want more than a partnership. I don't want to be two friends who got married because of a baby. Actually, that's not even still the same as it was when we first came up with this deal." She laughed without humor. "It's not a baby. It's a whole family that will be here in six months. Nothing is like it was when we cooked up the agreement. Especially not me."

"We agreed—"

"I know that!" Breathing in sharply, she tried to settle her stomach, which kept flipping over and back again, a little more violently each time she got more upset. "I didn't know we were having twins when I agreed. I had no idea what love looked like when I agreed. I had no idea that I'd experience such depths of feeling with you when I *agreed*. Emotions are not my forte. Don't you get that? This is hard for me and I was scared to bring it up because I don't know what I'm feeling."

Her hands shook with the effort to hold back the tears.

"Then you shouldn't have brought it up," he said flatly, refusing to look at her. "We had a line and you crossed it."

"I had to," she whispered, head bowed as something sharp tore through her chest. "I want more, Phillip. If you aren't willing to consider what I'm asking for, then I'm done here."

That got his attention. He glanced up abruptly. "What does that mean?"

"What it sounds like." An ending. What was ending, she wasn't sure. Her hopes? Her dreams? "I'm going to stay with Harper for a while until I can sort out what I want to do."

Drained, she rubbed at her temples, too shell-shocked to string together many more coherent words. Had they just broken up? Hard to say; she'd never done any of this before. She had no idea what came next, but what was happening at the moment was not something she could keep slogging through.

"I see." His eyebrows snapped together. "We agreed no love. We agreed no divorce. Apparently you're allowed to throw the entire agreement out the window if I don't bow to your wishes. Is that it? I have no say here?"

Divorce. The ugly word bit through her and something died inside. No, that wasn't what she wanted at all. But what was the alternative? They'd tried no expectations and that had been a dismal failure.

"I don't have the energy for this right now." That at least was the truth. "I have to think about the babies. I'm about to break into a million pieces and I'd prefer to do it somewhere you're not."

He nodded curtly. "Randy will take you to the airport. Fly home in my plane. Take care of yourself."

Too numb to cry, she gathered her bag and let Phillip help her into the car that would take her away from the man she suspected had just broken her heart.

Eleven

The next morning, Harper took one look at Alex's face and threw open the door of her Victory Park loft to embrace her. "Oh, honey. When you called, I had no idea it was that bad."

What was the definition of *bad*? That she didn't know whether she could be married to Phillip anymore? That he hadn't tried to stop her when she left? That in spite of everything, she'd fallen for her husband after all, and now that she knew love existed, it sucked?

Alex sniffed against Harper's shoulder. "It's bad. The worst part is that I don't even know why I'm crying."

The diminutive redhead herded Alex to the long off-white leather couch facing the Dallas skyline. A dozen floors below, traffic raced along the street, but up here, they were insulated from life's ebb and flow. If only the quiet would dull the riot of emotions seething through her stomach.

"You're crying because men are jerks and they should all be flayed alive with butter knives," Harper responded matter-of-factly. "Except Dante."

For some reason, that got a laugh from Alex. "Friends are exempt?"

Alex and Phillip had been friends once upon a time. Now they weren't even that. Were they? When she'd started this ill-advised descent into lunacy also known as admitting she cared for her husband, she should have thought it through a little better. Now she didn't have a friend, a partner *or* a father for her babies. That dull butter knife might be a kinder way to go.

Harper grinned fondly. "Dante's exempt because he's awesome and it would be a travesty for the world to lose his genius. The fact that he's one of the few people in the world who would drop everything for me is just a bonus."

That sounded so nice. She wanted Phillip to love her like that.

Stomach sloshing again, Alex groaned and leaned back against the couch. She'd flown back to Dallas last night and had been so sick by the time she got back to Phillip's house that she couldn't pack one single shirt, let alone all her belongings. She'd curled up on the bathroom floor, cheek to the marble, in hopes it would cool her tear-ravaged face or settle her stomach. It had done neither.

"I'm crying because of hormones. That's all," Alex assured Harper, though she'd stopped believing that at about three o'clock that morning. "This pregnancy is going to go down as the most difficult in history."

Harper snorted, reminding Alex she'd used the hormone excuse on her friend once already.

"I think all pregnant women say that. What's it feel like, anyway?"

"Like I drank four glasses of red wine, two shots of

Jägermeister and a gallon of Clorox in less than a minute. On an empty stomach."

Hormones weren't the reason she ached inside at the thought of never seeing Phillip again, never being held by him again. Not having that family with him that she'd envisioned where they woke up on a Saturday and went for brunch at a low-key restaurant, then swam in his parents' pool until it was time to get ready for one of Phillip's political fundraisers that evening. The kids would stay home with the nanny she'd hired with Connie's help, and in the car, Phillip would raise the privacy shield and turn to Alex with a wicked smile…

"Ha-ha." Her friend's nose wrinkled and she nodded to Alex's midsection. "I mean the being-pregnant part. You have real live babies in there. Is it weird?"

"Miraculous," she corrected and her heart thumped twice in rapid succession. Looked like that particular organ was still working after all. "They're mine. I'm the only person in the world who gets to have the experience of carrying them in my womb. When I give birth, they'll be my children forever and no one can take that away."

"Wow, your face just started glowing." Clearly fascinated, Harper zeroed in on it, her scientific brain no doubt cataloging all the nuances.

Alex didn't even have to think twice about how to describe it. "That's what love looks like."

The miracle, the energy Phillip had spoken of—that was how she felt about her babies. If nothing else, he'd given her the babies and they were a huge gift indeed.

"I'm a little jealous, honestly," Harper murmured, her smile faltering. "You and Cass are both moving to a new phase in life and I'm being left behind. Trinity is, too. I'm not sure she cares, though."

"But you care?" Alex eyed Harper but her vision was

still pretty blurry. Was she serious or just making conversation? "Since when do you think about being a mom?"

Harper shrugged, not even bothering to cover the wistfulness in her small smile. "Lately. It's not a crime."

The thought of Harper giving a man the time of day—let alone unbending enough to be intimate with one—was unfathomable. "Weren't we just talking about how men suck and should all be tortured?"

"Who needs a man? There are all sorts of ways to become a mother without introducing additional complexities like a relationship." As Alex well knew, and the point wasn't lost on her. The leather creaked under Harper's thigh as she crossed her legs. "You're going to be raising your babies alone, right? If you can do it, I could, too. We'll do it together."

Alone? As in without Phillip? *No.* That was not what was happening here. She'd needed breathing room, that was all. Her heart settled deeper in her chest as that reality clarified. She hadn't been able to pack because that wasn't the answer. She and Phillip were married. This was the part where it got hard but she'd made a commitment and she still wanted her babies to have a father. Phillip was the only one who got that title.

"Yeah, but the difference is that I don't want to be doing it alone. That's not what I'd envisioned for myself or my kids. At all."

So they'd have to find a way to make it work. Somehow. Her resolve faltered. Did that mean she'd have to go back to their original agreement and suck it up, never mentioning again the longings of her heart to have something more meaningful than a handshake?

"Well, it was just a thought, anyway." Leaning forward, she patted Alex's arm. "If you don't want to do it alone, then why are you here? Go back to Washington and work things out with Phillip. You had a great agreement going for you. Put it back together."

"It's not that simple," Alex wailed, her emotional threads bursting at the seams again. "Everything seemed so logical and reasonable and then I started wanting more, wanting things I don't even understand... He wasn't happy with me for bringing it up."

Of course he hadn't been. She'd broken the rules. Bad things happened when she did that, but she'd done it anyway. She was the poster child for letting selfishness guide her actions and then reaping what she'd sown.

Tossing her hair back, Harper narrowed her gaze. "Then I'm probably not the right person to help you sort it out. I love you like a sister but romantic love is a waste of time. When you said you and Phillip had a fight, I thought he'd brought up the issue about you working again."

"No, he got over that." Hadn't he? They'd never really talked about it again. More like it had been brushed under the carpet. Like everything else. "This is about our nontraditional marriage and whether I can keep being okay with it."

Phillip needed her and needed his marriage. That much she knew for a fact. He had his image to maintain, after all, she thought sourly.

"Then it sounds like you have some thinking to do about what you want to do. Of course, you're welcome to stay here until you figure it out." Brightly, Harper jumped up from the couch and held out her hand to help Alex to her feet. "Let's have some breakfast and you can fill me in on the status of the FDA application. As soon as we have approval, we're ready to gear up production of Formula-47, and frankly, I can't wait for two years' worth of work to come to fruition. Do I need to step in as Fyra's liaison now that things are dicey with Phillip?"

Alex groaned. The hearing on Monday. She'd forgotten all about it. The babies weren't the only reason she couldn't shed her relationship with Phillip quickly and easily, even if she wanted to. "The hearing is on Monday. I went to Washington yesterday with the sole intent to spend the weekend with Phillip and then go to the hearing, but instead, I ran away like a spoiled brat."

Some executive she was. In all her imaginings of her life with Phillip where they lived happily ever after with their family, her career hadn't entered the picture once. Because it was a given, she reminded herself fiercely. Fyra was her life.

Or at least it was right now. At some point in the future, she'd have two sweet babies added to the mix and she'd be a mother as well as a CFO. If she wanted to work things out with Phillip then she'd also be a wife, whatever that would look like.

And it was her job to deal with the FDA hearing. So she'd do it.

It was too much to contemplate and her morning sickness was back with a vengeance. So much so that she couldn't even think about breakfast. "I'll get the report from Phillip Monday night and fill you in. Don't worry about it."

Alex drifted through the rest of the weekend and somehow managed to sleep most of it. She was so tired, and Monday morning, she nearly called in sick. They'd filed the quarterly reports on Thursday last week; if there was ever a good time to take a break, this was it. But she hadn't taken one sick day since they'd opened the doors of Fyra, and now wasn't the day she'd start.

At three o'clock, an email popped into her inbox from the Office of Senator Edgewood and her heart did a slow dive, even though she knew before opening it that it was about the FDA hearing.

The committee is ready to move to the next step—touring the research facility. They'll expect to collect samples and research notes from the project. Talk to Harper and let me know when to schedule it. I'll be coming to Dallas with the committee as the liaison.

That was it. No mention of their fight or a question about how she was doing? Was that how it would be from now on? If so, she didn't like it. But she steeled her resolve and coordinated with Harper on a day and time later in the week. She responded to Phillip's email with the details, matching his businesslike tone. We'll expect you on Thursday, she wrote and hit Send.

As the week progressed, Alex's morning sickness grew to epic proportions. She barely kept down a few crackers and ginger ale, and she only ate that because Harper forced her to when Alex huddled on her friend's couch in the evenings, pretending to watch TV while the misery of her existence overwhelmed her.

She missed Phillip and couldn't stand things being so unsettled. That was the reason her stomach was so messed up. Her symptoms had improved last week or she would never have been able to go to Washington in the first place. Was this part of her punishment for daring to ask for more from her husband than a businesslike email as their sole communication in a week?

Thursday dawned as the worst day yet. Alex dragged herself from the froufrou coverlet on Harper's guest bed and forced herself into a pair of jeans that scarcely buttoned over her expanding stomach. Finally, she'd started outgrowing her clothes. Ironic that it had happened today of all days.

When the committee arrived at Fyra, Alex managed to be at the front, ready to greet them, though the dark-haired man in the center drew her gaze and kept it. Hungrily, she soaked up the sight of her husband, cataloging the fatigue around his eyes. He looked like he hadn't slept much and the thought lightened her heart at the same time it saddened her. She didn't want him to lose sleep over their situation. She wanted… Well, she wanted something that wasn't possible.

But what was possible? Could she agree to live with him again for the sake of the babies, in name only? She was sure he'd agree to go back to their original agreement. After all, becoming president one day guided all of his thoughts and actions. It was the whole reason they were married in the first place. If she wanted a father for her babies—and she did—could she forget about the fact that she'd fallen in love with him and he'd refused to reciprocate?

The answers did not arrive by way of osmosis simply by virtue of Phillip being within touching distance. The two men accompanying the senator introduced themselves and the tour started immediately thereafter. Harper met them at the door of the lab and took over to explain her setup and walk the committee through her processes. Which was a godsend, as Alex sincerely thought she might lose her breakfast of two crackers and ginger ale very shortly.

Phillip hung back, drawing near Alex, his blue eyes trained on her. "How are you doing?"

Tears pricked at her eyelids over the mere sound of his voice. "Not good. You?"

"Same." He shrugged. "I've been worried about you."

"I could tell from the way my phone never stopped ringing." A wave of dizziness cut off the rest of her sarcastic comment and she flung a hand out to steady herself, catching him square in the chest.

"Alex—" Phillip caught her in his strong arms as her

knees buckled. "What's happening? Talk to me, sweetheart."

"I...can't." Her tongue froze in panic as another wave of dizziness nearly blacked out her vision. If he hadn't been holding on to her, she would have hit the floor, no question. Something sharp tore through her abdomen. All the air rushed from her lungs as she fought to breathe, to understand, to keep her insides from falling out.

"The babies," she croaked and then blackness took her under.

Phillip had never known the true meaning of terror until the moment his wife passed out in his arms.

How he'd got her to the hospital in under twelve minutes remained a mystery he had no interest in solving. Not while everything that was precious to him hung in the balance.

Hospital personnel swarmed in and out of the triage area of the emergency room, taking vital signs and barking questions at him. He answered as best he could.

Yes, she was about fourteen weeks pregnant. No, he didn't observe anything unusual prior to the episode. Yes, she'd been complaining of an upset stomach. No, she hadn't been drinking alcohol or taking any kind of medication—that he knew of. Actually, the fact that he hadn't been right by her side every second had dug under his skin.

No matter what, he should have been there, taking care of his pregnant wife, not nursing the wounds of his black, conflicted heart.

One of the nurses escorted him from the room, very much against his will, as they began setting up a number of frightening machines and attaching them to Alex, who was lying on the hospital bed, skin as pale as the white sheets under her. What if she woke up and didn't know what was happening? Who would explain it to her? Who would hold her hand?

"Senator Edgewood, you have to clear the area and let us do our jobs," the nurse said firmly, leaving no doubt about whether his clout would have any sway here. It was a no.

He tried to take solace in the fact that the machines would help the competent doctors figure out what was wrong with his wife and assure everyone that the babies were fine.

They *were* fine. They had to be. Everyone was fine. Nothing else would be acceptable.

Time crawled to a halt as he sat in the waiting room, his head in his hands, partly because he couldn't hold it up and partly to keep anyone from recognizing him. Normally fame didn't bother him, but today he didn't want any questions about why he was in the emergency room… especially since he couldn't answer them. He had no idea what was wrong with his wife, because they weren't "together" right now.

Actually, he had no idea *what* they were. She hadn't called him, hadn't told him what she wanted to have happen next. Nothing. And he'd tried hard to honor her mandate that he give her space.

When he'd seen Alex again, it had been a punch to the throat—and then some. He'd been miserable since last Friday night. Miserable and unable to figure out what he was supposed to do to get what he wanted. And he'd had no idea how much he'd wanted her until he'd stood near Alex again, so close, yet unable to touch her like he longed to.

And then she'd been in his arms again, but not the way he'd dreamed. Oh, no. That swoon and faint was the stuff of nightmares.

Cassandra, Harper and Trinity rushed into the emergency room, heels clacking and dangly earrings sparkling with furious movement. The FDA tour must have concluded. He made a mental note to thank them all later for filling in the gaps his and Alex's absences had caused.

"What's going on?" Cassandra demanded before she'd even reached his chair.

Phillip shook his head. "I don't know yet. They haven't told me anything."

"And you're sitting there like a bump on a log?" Trinity scowled and swung around to terrorize the lady at the reception desk. They exchanged words, Trinity's rather heated, until finally, Fyra's chief marketing officer conceded defeat and returned to pace in the small waiting area off to the side where Phillip had chosen to set up camp.

After an eternity, a different nurse entered and approached Phillip. He shot to his feet, heart pounding as he braced himself for whatever news was about to be dropped. With Gina, he'd had no warning, no time to process. The authorities had come to his office personally to tell him, but she'd already been gone.

This was far worse because it was happening as he waited.

"Mrs. Edgewood is awake and asking for you," the nurse said without preamble.

Ten kinds of relief whooshed the air out of his lungs and he went a little light-headed. "What happened? Is she okay?"

The other three ladies clambered at his back, peppering the nurse with additional questions.

The nurse, who must have been used to the chaos of the waiting room, simply nodded. "She's stable. But she's dehydrated and her blood pressure was very low when she came in. We've got her on an IV."

The big, glaring omission in the status of Alex's situation iced Phillip's skin. "What about the babies? Everything's fine, right?"

The nurse's mouth firmed into a thin line. "There's a possibility of some…complications. We'll be running additional tests in the next few hours. I can't say anything else definitively at this time. You can go see her. Your wife is understandably very upset. It would be beneficial for her to relax if you can influence her."

With an apologetic backward glance at Alex's friends, he left them in the waiting room and followed the nurse through a maze of corridors to a different area than where Alex had started out.

Alex blinked up at him from the hospital bed, her skin ashen and her eyes huge and troubled. His heart went into a free fall and landed in the pit of his stomach. Mute, he stared at her as something cataclysmic shifted inside.

He could have lost her. And he knew what the pain would be like if that happened. He hadn't wanted to experience it again. But here he was, in the same exact boat despite all his efforts to the contrary. Despite all the pretending.

It would hurt to lose her.

Just like it hurt to be apart from her, and hurt to think about how his life would be meaningless if he didn't have Alex in it. He'd spent so much time shoving her away so he'd stay true to a promise he'd once made to another woman that he hadn't recognized it was already too late.

His problem wasn't that he didn't know how to get what he wanted—it was that he hadn't realized what he truly wanted until this moment.

Alex.

He was in love with Alexandra Edgewood. Letting her walk away last Friday might go down as the dumbest thing he'd ever done in his life. If he'd grabbed on to her with both hands, he could have been by her side all week as she'd grown sicker. He might have been able to fix things.

At the very least, neither of them would have spent the past week in misery.

Also his fault.

Weakly, she stretched out a few fingers, seeking his hand. "Phillip. What's happening?"

She wanted his comforting touch. The fact that she considered it such floored him. What did that mean? That it wasn't too late?

He obliged her by sliding a palm under hers, steeling his nerves so she didn't notice the shakes he'd developed in the past thirty seconds. How did you apologize for being such a moron when the woman you loved lay in a hospital bed, scared and upset? Squeezing her hand, he mustered a small smile.

"Everything's fine," he lied, which she obviously didn't believe for a second judging by the line that appeared between her eyes.

"They won't tell me what's happening with the babies." Alex bit her lip, a sure sign she had something on her mind she didn't know if she should say. "Dr. Dean is on her way. That can't be good."

"I'm sure that's standard procedure," he assured Alex with a composure he didn't feel in the slightest, but the nurse's admonition to keep Alex calm rang in his ears. "They're probably waiting on a qualified obstetrician to give her opinion."

"About what?" Alex asked tersely. "If nothing is wrong, then any doctor can look me in the eye and say that. I've felt so bad this week, but I thought it was because of...you know. What happened with us." Tears sprang up instantly in her green eyes, magnifying the brown dot that made her so unique. "I should have known something was wrong."

"Shh, you couldn't have known." Guilt settled a bit more

heavily across his shoulders. If only... "As for what happened between us, let's not worry about that now."

"I can't just not think about it," she whispered. "You were clear about the line I crossed. I've been ignoring the problems between us this week, obviously to my detriment. We have to figure out how to move forward."

Her gaze bored into him, convicting him. This was his wife to lose.

Maybe now was the perfect time to tell her how much of an idiot he'd been. "I was thinking the same thing."

"We have to consider the possibility that I might lose the babies." One tear slipped free from her eye and slid down her face. "I know we said no divorce and I agreed to that. But I have to know. If Dr. Dean gives us bad news, will you fight me on it?"

"Fight you on what?" Agape, he stared at her, his brain having an impossible time putting the horrific blocks of words together into something cohesive. And then it clicked. "You mean on granting you a *divorce*? Hell yes, I'll fight you on it. No divorce."

He couldn't lose her, especially not if the unthinkable happened and they left the hospital grief-stricken. The mourning process wasn't something you could do alone. He didn't want to do it alone and he didn't want her to grieve alone, either. They should be together. Always.

"Phillip, please." Her fingers curled around his, urgently digging into his flesh. "This is hard enough. Don't force me to stay in this marriage if there's no reason to. We only got married because of the babies. Why drag it out? I don't have the energy to indulge you in a lengthy battle, so I'm asking you point-blank if you'll agree."

"That's not the only reason we got married," he countered a bit desperately. "I—"

"I know." Her voice soured. "You have your voters to

consider. I get it. Well, I have my life to consider, too. I've had my eyes opened recently, and votes aren't my top priority. I'm sorry. I wish I could have stuck to the agreement, but things are changing. Honestly, I'm not even sure I can stay in this marriage if the babies are fine."

Misery turned her mouth down and he wanted to shut his eyes against it. "Alex, none of this has anything to do with votes. I'm trying to tell you I'm in love with you. Campaigns aside. I want to be married to you because of *you*. The babies are just an amazing bonus."

"What are you talking about?" Alex's expression grew hard. "Is this because I'm lying in a hospital bed? What happens tomorrow when I'm not in danger anymore? Once again, I'll be the convenient wife that isn't as good as your first one."

"Is that what you think?" God, he'd bungled this up but good. He squeezed his temples, wondering where all his stellar debate skills had flown off to. "I've never thought of you as second-best. You're actually better suited to me than Gina ever was."

That hadn't been what he'd planned to say. At all. But the words tumbled out, and as he heard himself say them, the truth became so clear. Gina had been wonderful but she hadn't challenged him. Alex made him better. Gina had been right for him once but Alex was right for the man he was now. A man he'd become because of Alex. A man who believed in second chances.

"You're not anything like her," he continued more strongly, determined to make up for some of the damage he'd done. "On purpose. I wanted you to be different so I could guarantee I'd never have feelings for you. But that's not how it went down. Instead, it just meant I could never compare you. I could certainly never find you lacking because you're perfect.

You don't blend into my world, which makes you unique and special. You stand out wherever you go. I love that about you."

That moment at the hospital ribbon cutting. When she'd tried so hard to speak to people, even though she'd been scared and uncomfortable and hadn't wanted to be there... that had probably been the moment when he'd fallen in love with her.

What had started as an attraction so fierce he'd dreamed about her pear scent for weeks had led him to a place he'd never imagined he'd be. In love again.

His promises to Gina had been slipping further away each day. He let them go, fully and irrevocably. His marriage to Gina was gone, but he had something wholly amazing in its place and he planned to embrace it.

Alex stared at the wall. "Too little, too late. You've had your chance to spout a bunch of pretty words. I think the only way to move forward is if we're not together."

Finally he knew what he wanted and she wasn't having any of it. "You're saying you want a divorce no matter what? I can't accept that."

"Well, guess what? I'm newly converted to the Phillip Edgewood philosophy of no second chances."

The phrase cut through him like a machete. Touché. And he totally deserved it.

A nurse bustled into the room, oblivious to how Phillip's entire world had just crashed down at the precise moment when he'd figured out exactly what he had to lose. If he hoped to keep the woman he loved, he had to go big.

Dr. Dean performed a lot of tests that took forever, but finally she declared the babies were fine. Alex breathed deeply for the first time since she'd awoken in the hospital bed.

At last it was over, and she still had two little heart-beats in her womb. The happy tears wouldn't stop cascading down her face, even though the rest of her life was in shambles.

A grim-faced Phillip had stuck by her bedside despite her telling him to go away several times. She got that he was concerned about the babies, so she didn't make a big deal out of it even though the echo of his beautiful voice saying *I love you* still pinged around inside her heart, looking for a place to latch on to.

She wasn't going to let it. No matter how much she wanted to believe it was real.

All of his declarations were an elaborate ploy to save face with his voters. He'd always cared more about appearances than she'd credited. She'd known when he brushed aside all her concerns about marriage that he'd needed her more than she'd needed him, but they'd gone far past reason and logic into something else entirely.

And to use her feelings against her—it was cruel and the height of emotional blackmail.

He could figure out how to spin the lack of a plus one whatever way he chose. She wasn't up for a repeat of the past few weeks, when she let herself believe he might be open to something more, only to be disappointed and heartbroken again. They'd have to figure out something else because she didn't want to be in this marriage any longer.

The irony of her choice to end their marriage wasn't lost on her. The one thing Alex had never wanted would come to pass because she'd dared to develop feelings for her husband.

Once she was released from the hospital, Phillip insisted on having Randy drive her home. But after a few minutes, she realized the car was traveling in the direction of Phillip's home, not Harper's, where she'd been staying.

"Randy." She tapped on the glass, only to have Phillip

snatch her hand back. She glared at her husband. "Are you kidnapping me, then?"

Figured. His dictatorial side had come out in spades.

"No." He scowled. "You just had a very serious episode. You need someone at your beck and call, twenty-four hours a day. *Me.* Harper will be busy with the FDA committee and unable to provide you with the care you need."

Yeah, Alex had heard that one before. He liked to "take care" of her all right; seduction was his favorite method to gloss over issues. Besides, as far as she knew, he'd been planning to fly back to Washington after the FDA committee tour. "That'll be a bit difficult for you to do when you'll be in another state. I can take care of myself."

Crossing her arms, she sank down in the seat. Residual wooziness hadn't worn off yet and she was so tired. Physically, mentally, spiritually.

"That's where you're wrong." He pulled his phone out and tapped a few times, then handed it to her.

She sighed, and even though she swore she wasn't going to humor him, she glanced at the screen anyway because why not? Blinking, she read over the words again. "That says you're taking an extended leave of absence. Until further notice. Phillip, you can't do that!"

"I can. And I did."

He pocketed the phone and gathered her hand in his carefully, as if handling something delicate and breakable. Since she wasn't quite sure which way was up at this point, she let him. And yeah, she still craved his touch, as much as she'd like to deny otherwise.

"But you're an elected official," she reminded him, unnecessarily, no doubt. "What's going to happen to your seat?"

"It's unpaid leave, so no taxpayers will feel defrauded. As long as I go back within the four weeks I was granted, my seat shouldn't be an issue. The biggest hit will be to goodwill. When I run for president, it will come up. I have no idea how damaging it'll be or how voters might view it." He shrugged. "But I don't care. This is more important. I want to spend time with you, pamper you. Eat meals with you."

Damaging? He'd deliberately take a leave of absence that might hurt his campaign for president? Oh, goodness. That was his brass ring. The most important thing in his life. Or at least it *used* to be. And he'd possibly thrown it all in the scrap heap for *her*.

Her greedy, traitorous heart soaked up the idea of being the center of Phillip's whole world and wouldn't let it go.

Dumbfounded, she scrabbled for something to say. And then reality set in. "Let me get this straight. You'll be here in Dallas. For four weeks. So this is a kidnapping disguised as a way to get me to take time off work?"

A double whammy. He wanted to be around to dictate her schedule so his babies were guaranteed safety.

"Alex."

She glanced at him and did a double take at his fierce expression.

"Don't make this about something other than what it is," he said. "You're pregnant with my children. I want to take care of you. When you feel better, go back to work. Or don't—I don't care. I trust that you'll make the right decisions *for you* because you're a smart person. Period, end of story."

"Really?" She eyed him. "We never established your expectations for my career. Long term. So you're okay with it if I hire a nanny and don't take off six months like you dictated?"

Madness. Why did she care? She was through with this

relationship, through with Phillip and through with trying to figure out why love was such an elusive beast.

Why did the thought of giving up make her heart hurt so badly?

"Completely. It's your choice."

He seemed so sincere, she wavered. What if her *if only* wish was actually coming true and she didn't give him a chance? One could argue she was just as bad as Phillip if she refused to give him a second chance. One could also argue that if she fell for his charm again, she was getting in line to be emotionally trounced.

She shook her head and opted to call a spade a spade. "You're just saying that so I'll change my mind about the divorce."

"When did you arrive at the conclusion that I'm someone who just tells you what you want to hear so I can get my way?" Clearly annoyed, he gripped her hand tighter. "That's the reason we're currently separated. Because I didn't do that. I've always been painfully honest with you, Alex. If I was going to lie to you in order to keep you, wouldn't a better time to do it have been that night in my Washington condo? I could have said I was falling for you then and avoided all of this. I didn't because I'm not like that."

"Uh—" Speechless, she replayed that point in her head and came up blank. "So what is all of this about, then?"

Tenderly, he smiled and cupped her face. "What I've been trying to tell you. I'm a big dummy who let some rules get in the way of what was happening between us. I didn't want to be hurt again. I lost someone I loved and I wasn't about to allow myself to go through that again. I set up the perfect scenario to make sure love was off the table, only I didn't count on you."

"What did I do?" she whispered. His warmth spilled

through her whole body, settling her nerves, her stomach, her heart.

"You kicked my rules to the curb and made me realize our agreement isn't worth the paper it's written on."

"Our agreement isn't written down," she pointed out through a throat so tight she could hardly breathe. Was he saying what she thought he was saying—that she'd broken the rules and *it was okay*?

He shrugged. "Guess there's nothing to rip up, then, in order to make way for our new agreement."

She didn't want to know. She *didn't*.

Oh, who was she kidding? "Which is?"

"Our marriage will be based on love. For better or worse. I solemnly swear that I'll spend the next fifty or sixty years giving us second, third, fourth, hell, as many chances as we need."

Maybe it really was this simple. Maybe she'd been right to open herself up to this man.

Her heart swelled. "What about divorce? Is that an option?"

"Never." Punctuating the statement by enfolding her into his arms, he smoothed her hair back as he gazed at her with something she'd swear was love in his eyes. "We're going to have the kind of marriage that lasts because I got lucky enough to find my soul mate a second time. No more talk of divorce."

It was real. This was what love looked like for her. It wasn't like in sappy movies or even what it looked like for Cass and Gage. Alex had never felt giggly and starry-eyed over a man because that wasn't who she was. The way she felt about Phillip was deep, lasting and so very real. And wonder of wonders, it seemed as if he'd fallen in love with her, as well.

"That sounds like an agreement I can get behind," she whispered through another round of happy tears.

He shook his head. "No, that was the part where you were supposed to say, 'Phillip, I love you, too. You're the best husband in the whole world. How could I ever live without you?'"

"Don't push your luck." She smiled at his mock scowl. "I do love you. Unexpectedly. Despite not even believing in it. Where did that come from?"

She knew. Phillip had demonstrated it from the first. She'd learned from him about what was possible.

"I'm very lovable. Did I forget to tell you?"

And then he kissed her as the town car turned onto the street where their house sat, silent and waiting for the laughter of the family that would live there for a very long time.

Epilogue

Harper put both hands on the conference table and leaned forward, looking very much like a redheaded pit bull in a Keith Lloyd suit. "What do you mean, the committee has questions about the formula samples?"

One hand on her expanding stomach, Alex glanced at Phillip and he took the question.

"As you know, they collected samples while they were here last month," Phillip interjected smoothly. "I'm sure it's just a formality. But they want to get additional samples because there was some question about possible tainting."

"What the hell does that mean?" Trinity piped in, finally glancing up from the ad copy that had dominated her attention thus far during the board meeting Alex and Phillip had called to discuss the progress of the FDA approval process. Or rather, the lack of progress. The committee's report had not included approval as those around this boardroom table had expected.

"It means they're suspicious about my lab," Harper threw in, steam nearly shooting from her ears as her Irish got up. "They think there's something dubious about my methods. Or something."

"No one is saying that," Alex said calmly as Phillip took her hand under the table to rub at one of her knuckles absently. He did that a lot. Random touching for no reason. And she reveled in it each time. "They just want to be sure before they approve the product. No harm in that."

"We still don't have a name attached to the leak." All heads turned toward Cass as she took control of the meeting. "That's the biggest concern when we start talking about a delay. Is the additional sample request negotiable, Phillip?"

"No. Sorry."

"Then we comply. Period." Cass held up her hand as Harper bowed up as if about to take on the entire front line of the Dallas Cowboys by herself. "Harper. Take five. Actually, let's all take a few minutes. Each one of us has an emotional stake in Formula-47."

The smile on Alex's face grew wide as she internalized the truth of that. Yes, she did. After all, it had brought her Phillip and the two babies in her womb that grew a little more each day. Who would have thought that she'd credit one of Fyra's products as the sole reason for all the wonderful things in her life?

In the hall, Phillip drew Alex into his embrace, his hand automatically smoothing across the swell of her abdomen. Instantly, one of the babies bumped against his palm.

"Oh! Did you feel that?" Alex's gaze flew to Phillip's and she was pretty sure the awe spreading across his face was mirrored in her own. "That was the first kick. And you got to feel it. How amazing is that?"

His four-week leave was nearly over and they'd already

decided that Alex would work remotely from Washington full-time once he went back to work. They couldn't stand to be apart for even a day. And when the babies were born, Alex had elected to take six months' leave from her job, during which she'd hire a nanny who would become well acquainted with the benefits of pictures and video.

"Miraculous," he murmured and pressed more firmly. "Just like you."

Fyra's Formula-47 wasn't the sole reason she had everything she'd never known she wanted. All the wonderful things in her life had to do with one simple act—breaking the rules.

* * * * *

Don't miss any of the stories in the
LOVE AND LIPSTICK *series*
from So You Think You Can Write *winner*
Kat Cantrell

THE CEO'S LITTLE SURPRISE
A PREGNANCY SCANDAL

And pick up these other sexy, fun reads
from Kat Cantrell

MARRIAGE WITH BENEFITS
THE THINGS SHE SAYS
PREGNANT BY MORNING

***

If you're on Twitter, tell us what you think
of Harlequin Desire! #harlequindesire

Available July 5, 2016

#2455 THE BABY INHERITANCE
Billionaires and Babies • by Maureen Child
When a wealthy divorce attorney unexpectedly inherits a baby, he asks the baby's temporary guardian to become a temporary *nanny*. But living in close quarters means these opposites can't ignore their attraction...by day or by night!

#2456 EXPECTING THE RANCHER'S CHILD
Callahan's Clan • by Sara Orwig
A millionaire rancher bent on revenge clashes with his beautiful employee, who is determined to do the right thing. Their intense attraction complicates everything...and then she becomes pregnant with his baby!

#2457 A LITTLE SURPRISE FOR THE BOSS
by Elizabeth Lane
Terri has worked for—and loved—single father Buck for years, but as the heat between them builds, so does Buck's guilt over a dark secret he's keeping from Terri. And then she discovers a little secret of her own...

#2458 SAYING YES TO THE BOSS
Dynasties: The Newports • by Andrea Laurence
With CEO Carson Newport and his top employee, PR director Georgia Adams, spending long hours together at the office, the line between business and pleasure blurs. But his family's scandals may challenge everything he knows and unravel the affair they've begun...

#2459 HIS STOLEN BRIDE
Chicago Sons • by Barbara Dunlop
For his father, Jackson Rush agrees to save Crista Corday from the con man attempting to marry her and steal her fortune—by kidnapping her from her own wedding! But he didn't count on wanting the bride for himself!

#2460 THE RENEGADE RETURNS
Mill Town Millionaires • by Dani Wade
An injury has forced rebel heir Luke Blackstone back home for rehabilitation...with the woman he scorned years ago. Determined to apologize, and then to seduce the straitlaced nurse, will the man who's made running away a profession stay?

———

YOU CAN FIND MORE INFORMATION ON UPCOMING HARLEQUIN® TITLES, FREE EXCERPTS AND MORE AT WWW.HARLEQUIN.COM.

HDCNM0616

REQUEST YOUR FREE BOOKS!
2 FREE NOVELS PLUS 2 FREE GIFTS!

H HARLEQUIN®

Desire

ALWAYS POWERFUL, PASSIONATE AND PROVOCATIVE

YES! Please send me 2 FREE Harlequin® Desire novels and my 2 FREE gifts (gifts are worth about $10). After receiving them, if I don't wish to receive any more books, I can return the shipping statement marked "cancel." If I don't cancel, I will receive 6 brand-new novels every month and be billed just $4.55 per book in the U.S. or $5.24 per book in Canada. That's a savings of at least 13% off the cover price! It's quite a bargain! Shipping and handling is just 50¢ per book in the U.S. and 75¢ per book in Canada.* I understand that accepting the 2 free books and gifts places me under no obligation to buy anything. I can always return a shipment and cancel at any time. Even if I never buy another book, the two free books and gifts are mine to keep forever.

225/326 HDN GH2P

Name	(PLEASE PRINT)

Address	Apt. #

City	State/Prov.	Zip/Postal Code

Signature (if under 18, a parent or guardian must sign)

Mail to the **Reader Service:**
IN U.S.A.: P.O. Box 1867, Buffalo, NY 14240-1867
IN CANADA: P.O. Box 609, Fort Erie, Ontario L2A 5X3

Want to try two free books from another line?
Call 1-800-873-8635 or visit www.ReaderService.com.

* Terms and prices subject to change without notice. Prices do not include applicable taxes. Sales tax applicable in N.Y. Canadian residents will be charged applicable taxes. Offer not valid in Quebec. This offer is limited to one order per household. Not valid for current subscribers to Harlequin Desire books. All orders subject to credit approval. Credit or debit balances in a customer's account(s) may be offset by any other outstanding balance owed by or to the customer. Please allow 4 to 6 weeks for delivery. Offer available while quantities last.

Your Privacy—The Reader Service is committed to protecting your privacy. Our Privacy Policy is available online at www.ReaderService.com or upon request from the Reader Service.

We make a portion of our mailing list available to reputable third parties that offer products we believe may interest you. If you prefer that we not exchange your name with third parties, or if you wish to clarify or modify your communication preferences, please visit us at www.ReaderService.com/consumerchoice or write to us at Reader Service Preference Service, P.O. Box 9062, Buffalo, NY 14240-9062. Include your complete name and address.

HDI5

*With CEO Carson Newport and his top employee, PR
director Georgia Adams, spending long hours together at
the office, the line between business and pleasure blurs.
But his family's scandals may challenge everything he
knows and unravel the affair they've begun...*

Read on for a sneak peek at
SAYING YES TO THE BOSS
the latest installment in the
DYNASTIES: THE NEWPORTS *series*
by *Andrea Laurence*.

"To the new Cynthia Newport Memorial Hospital for
Children!" Carson said, holding up his glass. "I really can't
believe we're making this happen." Setting down his cup, he
wrapped Georgia in his arms and spun her around.

"Carson!" Georgia squealed and clung to his neck.

When he finally set her back on the ground, both of them
were giggling and giddy from drinking the champagne on
empty stomachs. Georgia stumbled dizzily against his chest
and held on to his shoulders.

"Thank you for finding this," he said.

"I know it's important to you," she said, noting he still
had his arms around her waist. Carson was the leanest of
his brothers, but his grip on her told of hard muscles hidden
beneath his expensive suit.

In that moment, the giggles ceased and they were staring
intently into each other's eyes. Carson's full lips were only
inches from hers. She could feel his warm breath brushing
over her skin. She'd imagined standing like this with him so
many times, and every one of those times, he'd kissed her.

Before she knew what was happening, Carson pressed his lips to hers. The champagne was just strong enough to mute the voices in her head that told her this was a bad idea. Instead she pulled him closer.

He tasted like champagne and spearmint. His touch was gentle yet firm. She could've stayed just like this forever, but eventually, Carson pulled away.

For a moment, Georgia felt light-headed. She didn't know if it was his kiss or the champagne, but she felt as though she would lift right off the ground if she let go. Then she looked up at him.

His green eyes reflected sudden panic. Her emotions came crashing back down to the ground with the reality she saw there. She had just kissed her boss. Her boss! And despite the fact that he had initiated it, he looked just as horrified by the idea.

"Georgia, I…" he started, his voice trailing off. "I didn't mean for that to happen."

With a quick shake of her head, she dismissed his words and took a step back from him. "Don't worry about it," she said. "Excitement and champagne will make people do stupid things every time."

The problem was that it hadn't felt stupid. It had felt amazing.

Don't miss a single story in Dynasties: The Newports
Passion and chaos consume a Chicago real estate empire

SAYING YES TO THE BOSS
by Andrea Laurence, available July 2016!

And
AN HEIR FOR THE BILLIONAIRE by Kat Cantrell
CLAIMED BY THE COWBOY by Sarah M. Anderson
HIS SECRET BABY BOMBSHELL by Jules Bennett
BACK IN THE ENEMY'S BED by Michelle Celmer
THE TEXAN'S ONE NIGHT STAND-OFF by Charlene Sands
Coming soon!

www.Harlequin.com

Whatever You're Into... Passionate Reads

Looking for more passionate reads from Harlequin®?
Fear not! Harlequin® Presents, Harlequin® Desire and
Harlequin® Blaze offer you irresistible romance stories
featuring powerful heroes.

♦ HARLEQUIN *Presents*

Do you want alpha males, decadent glamour and jet-set
lifestyles? Step into the sensational, sophisticated world of
Harlequin® Presents, where sinfully tempting heroes ignite a
fierce and wickedly irresistible passion!

♦ HARLEQUIN *Desire*

Harlequin® Desire novels are powerful, passionate and
provocative contemporary romances set against a backdrop of
wealth, privilege and sweeping family saga. Alpha heroes with
a soft side meet strong-willed but vulnerable heroines amid a
dramatic world of divided loyalties, high-stakes conflict and
intense emotion.

♦ HARLEQUIN *Blaze*

Harlequin® Blaze stories sizzle with strong heroines and
irresistible heroes playing the game of modern love and lust.
They're fun, sexy and always steamy.

Be sure to check out our full selection of books
within each series every month!

www.Harlequin.com